Christmas of Love

24 MILLIONAIRES, BILLIONAIRES, ALPHA MALES AND FEMALES, WORKPLACE ROMANCES, FRIENDS TO LOVERS, INSTALOVE, SWEET ROMANCES.

MARINA PACHECO

MARINA PACHECO

Contents

Sign up for Marina Pacheco's no-spam newsletter that only goes out when there is a new book or freebie available and get my free collection of short stories!

Details can be found at the end of this book.

1st December

ANNA & HER FRAGRANT PROTECTOR

'Oh, this is such a nice place, Anna,' mom says as she guides me through the automatic doors of the Ocean Breeze Hotel.

They open with a mechanical swoosh and envelop us in warmth and the smooth sounds of Christmas jazz. Mom has a light grip on my left elbow, more a touch than a hold. It's something we've perfected over the years so we don't make it obvious she's leading me, although my white stick is a dead giveaway.

'I've never seen a lobby like it.' Mom's voice drops to a conspiratorial whisper. 'It's two storeys, with this amazing double spiral staircase that looks like it's floating upwards with a modern tubular crystal chandelier plunging right through the middle. The whole facade is glass with a fantastic view of the ocean. The receptionists must love working here because they're facing outwards. The reception, by the way, is a long s-shaped desk at the back. It's quiet now, but they've got three people on duty, two women and a man.'

My mom's descriptive abilities have improved over the last few years. When I first lost my sight, she was just about the facts, saying things like, 'The room is 100m wide and 50m deep. There are twelve coffee tables on the right, each with four club chairs. The floor is white marble.' All relayed in an anxious, almost robotic tone as if she was afraid to miss anything out. It was awful and made me feel bad.

Now she relishes this role, although she gets to do it less frequently as I have learned to navigate through the world. But today is one of those days when I need her.

'This looks like a great place to work.'

Mom sounds relieved. I didn't even tell her I was going for the interview, not till it was over. I was nervous enough as it was and she would have been too. To be honest, I was surprised to get the job.

I'm a masseuse. My clients, once they get used to the idea that I'm blind, tell me I have magic hands. But I couldn't convince any of the spas and health centres along the coast up to Cascais. Being blind put them off. They always listed all the potential problems and didn't listen when I pointed out the benefits.

So I've been eking out a living taking clients at our little apartment. It wasn't ideal, especially when one of my clients, who was creepy to begin with, started groping me. Mom had to call the police to force him to leave. She says she's never seen him again but I'm not sure that's true. It bothers me that he knows where we live and that there is only me and mom at home.

Still, no need to worry now. I finally landed a job, astonishingly, at the poshest hotel and spa in Cascais. Maybe it helped that I had to give a massage as part of the process. Funnily enough, it was the first time an interviewer has asked me to do that. Maybe it was that I'd never got far enough on previous attempts.

'I was told to go to reception.'

Mom already knows, but my nerves have kicked in making me repeat myself.

'It's straight down from the main entrance for about fifty steps,' mom says. 'Then veer diagonally to your right and you'll be at reception.'

Normally, I would have come to the hotel a couple of days before to pace the whole thing and get my bearings, but everything happened so quickly that I couldn't fit in a visit. All I have is the interview day, when I had somebody from Vision to support me and help me find the basics like the interview room and the toilets.

Vision is a godsend. They're a charity that supports the blind. When I lost my sight, they helped me regain my autonomy. They're also lobbyists for blind people, and provide support for people when they need it, like help to attend an interview. They even offered to come with me this morning, but it wasn't necessary. Mom would have fought them for this opportunity. It makes her feel better knowing where I'll be working.

My stick makes contact with a glass barrier and I don't need mom's whispered, 'Reception.'

'Excuse me?' I say.

I've perfected a way of calling for attention that hopefully isn't too intrusive if the staff are all busy.

'Yes, ma'am, how can I help you?' a professionally pleasant middle-aged woman asks.

'It's my first day at work.' I can't help the proud note in my voice. 'My name is Anna Ramos. I'm the new masseuse.'

'Ah, welcome, Miss Anna. I'll just look up your details.'

Computer keys clack away, and I turn to mom. She's let go of my arm, but I can still smell the light floral perfume that she always wears so I can find her, mingled with her fabric softener and the soft powdery smell of her I've always loved.

'I'll be fine on my own now,' I whisper.

'Are you sure?'

I nod emphatically. 'You've got to get to work, too.'

'I took the morning off.'

'Might as well go now, though.'

If mom isn't around, she doesn't get paid, so it's better if she gets to work early. She knows it too. She takes me gently by the shoulders, turns me slightly and I feel her soft velvety skin brush my cheeks as she gives me a farewell kiss to each side.

'You'll tell me all about it when you get home, won't you?'

'Of course.'

I listen to her click clack away, making sure she definitely leaves and doesn't just hover out of range, checking on me. The automatic door swishes open and then closed. Now I really am on my own.

'Here you go,' the receptionist says. People forget the blind can't read name badges so they rarely introduce themselves and I don't have the courage today to ask. I hear something metallic and plastic clunk onto the counter. 'This is your staff ID. It also has the key card to let you into the employees' section of the spa.'

'Thank you,' I say and feel forward till I find the ID. It feels like a lanyard is wrapped around it. I carefully unwind it, getting a sense of the shape of the thing and which end is which.

Some people rush to help, usually over the wrong things, others behave as if I'm not blind at all. I think this receptionist is the latter.

'Could you direct me to the staff entrance, please?'

'I'll get a porter to show you the way,' the receptionist says, but she sounds unimpressed. 'You won't be able to rely on them all the time, you know?'

'Do you not show any other new members of staff around?'

I ask partly because one should never assume, but also because she sounds like one of those people who thinks the disabled should cause less trouble by just staying at home.

'Manuel,' the receptionist says so loudly it makes me jump.

'Yes, ma'am,' a male voice says.

The horribly familiar voice of my groper.

'Help Miss Anna to the spa reception. They can take her from there.'

'Oh, um, I think I can get there on my own,' I say. 'I went there for my interview.'

I've come over in a cold sweat. I can't believe this man actually works at my new dream job.

'No need to worry,' Manuel says and I can hear the relish in his voice. He probably can't believe his luck. 'I'll take you right inside.'

He wraps his arm around my waist and pulls me closer as his fingers dig into my side.

'No,' I say, and try to pull away. 'I've been there before. I'm can find my own way, really.'

Manuel's grip tightens, and he says close to my ear, 'Let's get on well as co-workers, shall we? No need to be stuck up.'

'I'm not stuck up. You're too close.'

I push at him, but his grip is far too tight.

'Manuel?' the receptionist says, doubt in her voice.

'It's alright, I know her. She's my masseuse.'

'I am not!' I shout and push away from him with all my might.

He lets go and I stagger into the unknown, off balance, flailing, falling backwards. I expect to crash into furniture or land on the floor. Instead, an arm wraps about me, somebody strong who feels tall, who straightens me up and makes sure I'm steady.

'Are you alright?' a cool clipped, posh male voice asks.

I breathe in his cologne: a nose full of salty ocean and cool menthol and memory floods in.

It's the 1st of December, just like today. I'm eighteen, standing in the Cais do Sodré Train station. It's filled with the echoing sound of commuters, traffic outside, trains inside and a group playing Christmas carols with fiddles and an accordion. I'm paralysed, alone in the middle of this crush, waving my white stick warily. I've been pointed in the right direction, but this is my first solo voyage and my heart is beating so hard I can feel it to my fingertips.

I take one hesitant step, and then another. Twenty-three steps to the ticket barrier. I pace them out, one, two... a fifth step and wham, somebody crashes into me, mutters an apology and vanishes. I'm gasping for breath, shaken, and then I realise I've dropped my stick.

'Help!' I say, but not loudly.

I'm too embarrassed that I can't even do this one thing of finding my own stick. I feel forward with my foot but find nothing. So I bend down. I remember how filthy the cobbles are in this station from my sighted days. It feels gritty and damp as I grope about, praying nobody else collides with me now that I'm down and vulnerable.

'Here,' a brusque young man says, grabs one questing hand and pushes my stick into it.

'Thank you,' I gasp, clutching the stick with both hands just to make sure.

'What are you doing out here on your own?' He sounds like he's my age and he smells really nice, fresh like the ocean and something... maybe minty. 'Where do you need to go?'

'It's a test.' My face feels hot with shame. 'I have to get to Cascais on my own.'

'On your own? Is that even possible?'

'It is. I've been practising with my group. This is my first solo attempt and I want to succeed today.'

'Okay then,' he says and lets go.

'Wait,' I cry, feeling abandoned. 'Please just turn me to face the ticket barrier.'

'How's this doing things on your own?' his voice snaps from just behind me.

'I'm allowed to ask for help. I'm not stupid.'

He grips my shoulders tighter than is warranted and rotates me about 30 degrees.

'Just walk straight ahead, maybe... fifteen steps.'

'Thanks,' I say, and because I know he's watching, I step forward more boldly than I could on my own.

Fifteen paces on, exactly, I come to the barrier and I get the same waft of ocean cologne so I know he's come in right behind me. I pretend not to notice, but it feels like I'm cheating with this stranger watching over me.

I make it onto the train and stand holding a pole near the door. Nobody ever tells blind people if a seat is free, so I can't figure out where to sit and I'm feeling too bashful to speak up. While we're trundling along the line, I get a whiff of the same cologne. So my mysterious protector is still there.

Finally, I reach Cascais and the announcement that it's the end of the line and we all get off. I'm feeling more confident now. I've made it, I'm nearly there.

As I'm going through the ticket barrier on this end, I get another whiff of oceans. So he was there all the way. I don't have a chance to say anything because as I clear the gate, my mother comes running, calling my name and wraps me in a bear-hug, weeping tears of relief.

Later I noticed my stick smelled like my rescuer. I wished I could seal the scent in and keep it forever, but after a few days, it had faded.

Now, here I am in the lobby of a posh hotel, being held by...

'Excuse me,' I gasp, 'your cologne, I've smelled it before.'

'I doubt it,' the man says. 'My grandmother took me to some eccentric old woman in Sintra for a personalised scent. I'm the only one who has this.'

Confirmation then, although I was pretty sure already because I've never smelled the same thing since.

'Mr César!' somebody cries and I hear several people running towards me, or rather towards my rescuer.

'I'm fine,' he says and pulls my identification out of my hand.

'It's my first day,' I mutter and feel my face growing warm again.

'I see.' His voice is cold, impersonal, disinterested. 'You, João, see our new member of staff safely to her manager,' he says, and he pushes my ID back into my hand.

'Yes, sir, immediately, sir,' the man says and by the way his voice fluctuates, he sounds awed.

'And you,' César says, his tone instantly hard as ice. 'What do you mean by groping a woman in my foyer?'

'I was just trying to help, sir,' Manuel says, sounding terrified.

I try to imagine my rescuer's expressions. How scary must he be?

'We'd better go,' João murmurs and touches my elbow with what feels like exaggerated care.

'Women who are being helped,' César says, 'do not push men away with such force. Fetch your things and get out of my hotel.'

Manuel gasps. It feels like there's a collective shudder, but maybe that's my imagination. João speeds up.

'Best not to be around when the boss gets angry.'

'Is he the hotel manager?' I ask, moving too fast to make out much of Manuel's desperate protests and pleas to remain.

'He's the owner. You don't want to get on the wrong side of him. He's got a nasty temper.'

I'm amazed. This man has saved me twice in my life, that's quite the coincidence. He clearly terrifies his staff, but he'll always be my Christmas saviour.

2nd December

MARIA FEARS THE WORST

Bernardo looks tense and that worries me. We're dining at our favourite restaurant, the Sea and Sun, gazing out of the window onto the cliffs. His expression is so sombre you'd think there was a storm raging outside, but no, it's a beautiful sunny December day and the icy blue Atlantic water in merely lapping gently on the rocks below.

As it's a weekday lunchtime, only two-thirds of the tables are full. Everyone looks happier than we do, chatting away, smiling and one couple are holding hands across the table. It's just us who seem at a loss for words.

It was his idea to come out this way for lunch and now I'm wondering why. Stella, an old high school friend, is the head chef and owner. Maybe he feels he needs moral support. I'm just filled with gloom despite the view.

He'd said next to nothing on the drive over either, just gazed ahead, chewing on his bottom lip. I tried to distract myself by staring out onto the ocean for the hour-long drive, but I couldn't stop myself from sneaking glances at him all the way.

I wish he'd tell me what was wrong, but every time I ask, he just smiles and gives me a vague answer. He's been like this ever since his best friend, Armando, got married. No, actually, a little before that he'd started getting pensive and asking me questions he'd never asked before, like whether I was happy. That came out of the blue.

Bernardo is generally a cheerful man, which is why I'm so worried. He's almost the stereotypical big friendly bear, tall and chubby, which I sometimes tease him about, but only because I worry over his health. He's got wavy auburn hair that he keeps neat and short, and a darker beard which gives him gravitas. Although, when he's angry, he can be overwhelming. He has to be. He's the manager of his family's banks and always has to show he's in charge.

Today he's wearing tan trousers and a matching waistcoat, white long-sleeved shirt and a tan tweed jacket, but no tie. This is his version of dressing down and it usually means he's relaxed and looking forward to a nice day out. So why is he fidgety?

Whenever he looks this uncomfortable I put it down to Maria, his ex-wife. I have the misfortune of having the same name as someone I have no hesitation labelling an evil woman. She was married to Bernardo for five years and he loved her wholeheartedly.

I became his secretary a year into his marriage and liked him at once but not in the romantic sense. I was determined not to be that cliché of a secretary who intended to seduce and marry her boss. I had my pride, after all. As a capable woman, I was more than able to put a roof over my own head and food on my own plate. Thank you very much.

But it appalled me how Maria the first (small f, I'm not giving her any importance) treated him from day one. It wasn't outright disdain, but a subtle dismissiveness. I always got the sense that she was using her husband.

She certainly enjoyed spending his money. I know because I was the one who had to determine which expenses went through the books and which were theirs as a couple. This may sound simple, but when a wife has to accompany her husband to business lunches and fancy corporate events, then the buying of dresses, shoes and jewellery can be called a business expense. Maria the first wasn't beyond slipping in all sorts of additional purchases, though.

And then, out of the blue, Maria the first instigated an argument at a celebrity event, demanded a divorce and stormed out in dramatic fashion, ensuring maximum tabloid coverage. Bernardo was shocked and heartbroken that his wife wanted to leave him. He was even more stunned when he got the demand from her divorce lawyers for an eye-wateringly large settlement.

He might have given in, such was his state of despair, but for his inheritance. Bernardo has two younger brothers snapping at his heels, dying to take over the family business. I had never been more thankful for sibling rivalry, which I'd usually viewed as toxic, till that moment. It made Bernardo fight back.

There followed a bruising year long legal battle. After that, Maria the first flounced permanently out of Bernardo's life, considerably richer than when she'd married him but nowhere as rich as she'd wanted. Bernardo was devastated and I found myself looking after him far more than my role as secretary required.

Over time, without really noticing, we became a couple. It was low key at first, two people who were fond of each other but being cautious. Me, because I didn't want the world to know I was dating my boss. Bernardo because he'd been burned once and was wary of having the same thing happen again.

But gradually our tentative encounters became something deeper and stronger. I gave up holding my feelings back and fell deeply in love. Bernardo felt the same and finally asked if I wanted to move in with him, which I did.

I had no expectations of more, but over the last few years I've wanted to get married. I want to tell the world that I love this man and he loves me. But Maria the first looms over us like an ominous ghost. Bernardo won't even think about marriage, never mind actually walking me to the altar. Now here we are sitting in uncomfortable silence and I'm terrified about what it means.

'Hello, Bernardo, looking handsome as ever and Maria, always the most elegant woman I know,' Stella says, emerging from her kitchen flushed, but immaculate in her chef's hat, white shirt and black apron. 'How are my most glamorous lovebirds doing?'

Bernardo laughs and says, 'You mean your most loyal customers? I suspect you have far more spectacular couples than us.'

I blinked to hear him say something like that. Is he distancing himself from me?

'You're our favourite chef.'

I smile as warmly as I can, although I feel fake.

'Thank you.' Stella is beaming, as if she hasn't noticed how uncomfortable we are. 'Are you ready for your first course?'

I'm taken aback since I've barely had time to look at the menu. Bernardo catches my surprise and flushes.

'Actually, I took the liberty of arranging a meal ahead of time,' he says, tenser than ever. 'It's... a surprise.'

'You arranged a surprise?'

'I know.' He gives a rueful laugh as he runs a hand through his hair. 'I usually leave all the planning to you. But I wanted today to be different.'

I wish he'd sounded more confident as he spoke. It's not like Bernardo to look uncertain. It makes me uneasy.

Stella signals to the kitchen and the head waiter comes over and places a couple of plates of fresh oysters before us.

'Enjoy. I'll leave you two lovebirds to your meal,' Stella says, and off she goes.

'Oysters?' I ask, looking from my plate and the gleaming, plump shellfish to Bernardo. 'You don't even like oysters.'

'But you do... so, bottoms up,' he says, picks up an oyster and swallows it manfully.

Now I'm really confused. Why this fancy meal and why oysters, a known aphrodisiac? Although, knowing Bernardo, he's more likely to become green about the gills from downing oysters than titillated. Despite loving oysters, there is no way I'm going to enjoy it when I'm frustrated to the point of tears.

'Look, Bernardo, what exactly is going on?'

'Huh?' he says, which for him is evasive and alarms me even more.

'Exactly!' I say, waving an oyster shell at him, its contents dangerously close to slipping out and plopping onto the perfect white tablecloth. 'You've been so different lately. I can't take it anymore.'

'No, Maria... wait, calm down,' Bernardo says waving at me with both hands. 'I knew I was messing up.'

At least he knows. Bernardo is a sweet man, but not the best when it comes to understanding other people's feeling.

'The thing is,' Bernardo says, 'we've been together for eleven years, you know that?'

'Well... I wouldn't say together. I was just your secretary for the first four.'

'The best secretary I've ever had,' Bernardo says, beaming.

'Pretty much the only secretary you've ever had.' Thank god he looks calm, and even like he's beginning to relax. 'But why are you talking about how long we've been together?'

Is he trying to draw a line? Is this a farewell banquet? Does he want me out of his life? Farewell boyfriend, farewell job? Surely not, but if not, then why this elaborate meal and this conversation?

'Just enjoy your oysters,' Bernardo says, and pushes his plate towards me, 'and have as many of mine as you'd like too.'

Oysters are not the kind of thing you have as a takeaway, although at this point that's all I want to do with them, so that I can run away from this weird and uncomfortable situation.

I swallow mine just to get rid of them. I leave his. The waiter clears the plates without comment and brings the next dish. It's another of my favourites, and not usually found on Stella's menu: Alentejan pork and clam stew. It's delicious and any other day I'd be swooning with pleasure over each mouthful. Today I may as well be eating sawdust.

'We've had a good run, haven't we?' Bernardo says in the tones of somebody jollying on a reluctant companion.

'A good run?' I reply, my voice hollow.

This is it, this is really it. Nobody says things like this if they want to remain together.

'Well, you know, eleven years. It's longer than my first marriage, and the marriages of some of my friends.'

'So?' I say although it costs me effort, and I keep my head down, pretending I'm trying to decide between a clam or a succulent piece of pork. Why am I hastening the inevitable?

'So... maybe it's time for a change?' Bernardo leans forward and tilts his head so that he's looking up at me, his eyes wide and worried. At least he's not enjoying this either.

'Really, a change?' I'm trying hard not to cry. I can't believe this is happening, even though I've been fearing it for weeks. To finally be here is heart-breaking. I push my plate away. 'I'm not really in the mood for food.'

'Are you unwell?' Bernardo asks immediately alarmed.

A part of me wants to say, yes, I'm ill. Can we do this another day? But I can't be that much of a coward. If Bernardo has fallen out of love with me, what can I do? I have to be grown up and gracious, and accept it. You can't change somebody's heart after all, no matter how much pain it causes you.

'I think we should move onto the dessert,' I say, giving him my brightest smile.

'Of course.'

Bernardo is looking increasingly alarmed as he signals for the waiter.

I'm expecting Stella's signature dish of a gooey chocolate pão de ló with salted caramel sauce. Instead, the waiter wheels out a large cake, covered in snow white frosting and surrounded by the most perfect ring of roses. The waiter comes to a halt before us and starts lighting the mass of candles which just throws me as it isn't my birthday and Bernardo doesn't make mistakes like this. But it's also just too much for a breakup.

Then Bernardo crosses to my side and goes down on one knee, the flames of the candles looking like a halo behind him.

Oh, I think, did I get this all wrong?

'Maria.' Bernardo clears his throat. 'I know I've been damned slow getting to this point, and you have shown the patience of a saint. But today...' Bernardo reaches into his pocket, 'will you forgive me for being so indecisive and agree to marry me?'

He flips open a small blue velvet box edged in gold. Inside is a simple ring with a twinkling solitaire diamond.

'Oh!' I gasp. Tears well up and I smack his shoulder over and over. 'You foolish man! I thought you were going to break up with me!'

'Break up with you!?' Bernardo says and leaps to his feet. 'Why on earth would I break up with you?'

'You've been so distant lately,' I say, sniffing and wiping under my eye to catch the tears. 'I thought you didn't love me anymore.'

'You should know me better than that.' Bernardo pulls me to my feet and folds me into a gentle embrace, resting his chin on my head. 'I'm exactly like a bear, you know. When I've got a big decision to make, I curl up in the dark and do my deep thinking. I'm sorry I didn't realise how much that undermined your confidence.'

'I know that,' I mumble into his reassuring warm chest, ignoring that everyone in the restaurant has turned to watch us. 'I should know that. You've done it before but usually for work and never towards me.'

'I'll work on giving you fair warning when I'm off to hibernate again,' Bernardo says, and leans back so he can see my face. 'So, what do you say? Will you marry this hopelessly slow man?'

'I will,' I say and heave a great sigh of relief as Bernardo slips the ring onto my finger.

The shock of the moment is fading and I can give in to the deep, wonderful feeling that Bernardo really does love me, so much that he's overcome his fears and proposed. And he's currently grinning and waving to the crowd of interested onlookers who've broken into applause as if he's just won the Grand Prix.

Well, maybe he has, I think, as I lean up and give him a kiss that he returns wholeheartedly. I know I have.

3rd December

FRANCINE REMAINS SINGLE

'I brought lunch,' my boss, Luca, says as he lets himself into my apartment holding a plastic bag out for inspection.

I say boss, but he's more than that. We've known each other since I was fourteen and he was sixteen. We've been best friends for nearly two decades and he was the only one to take me seriously when I said I wanted to transition from modelling to business.

'I am perfectly able to look after myself, you know,' I say without shifting from the sofa.

I've twisted my ankle so badly the doctor ordered me to stay in bed and keep my foot elevated for six weeks. Thank god it wasn't broken. Luca smiles and looked at me for the first time and, as expected, his perfectly plucked and shaped eyebrows rise nearly to the roof.

'What's with the turban? Are you channelling the 80s?'

'My hair's filthy and I can't shower easily, so I'm just hiding it.'

'From whom?'

I've had some seriously jealous boyfriends in the past, but thankfully Luca isn't one of them. We had a brief fling in our early twenties, but by that stage I was already moving out of the idea of finding a soulmate and support for life. Maybe if he'd approached me earlier, things might have been different. But Luca has baggage of his own.

For a start, he's the most beautiful man I've ever seen. Not handsome, mind you, although if he dressed in a manly way, he might well be considered handsome. But Luca is into women's clothing. I don't think it's surprising, considering he grew up in one of the most prestigious fashion houses in Milan surrounded by gorgeous gowns. He has the height and slim build to carry it off to o.

He used to drive his father mad, trying on the dresses for their fashion house's shows. His father was a typical overbearing, macho Italian man. He took what he wanted whenever he wanted and that included any model he took a fancy to.

That was how we met, when Luca punched his father so hard he knocked him right off my struggling self, who'd been pinned to a table. His father hit him back so hard he'd crashed through two clothes rails, tearing hellishly expensive creations as he windmilled through them.

And so they continued, Luca and his dad, coming to blows every day over women and how Luca liked to dress. Today he's gone with a simpler look, a long deep blue chenille jumper over skin-tight jeans, and only a natural-looking touch of makeup.

'Alright,' he says, shaking his head at my slovenly attire. I haven't even bothered to get out of my pyjamas, although they are silk. 'Before I make you lunch, I'll wash your hair.'

I'm about to tell him not to bother but my itchy my scalp is driving me crazy.

'Okay, if you insist,' I say, feigning reluctance.

Luca shakes his head as he helps me up and, with one arm draped over his shoulder, I hop to the bathroom. Luca guides me to the plastic chair I've set up in the shower. It's tight in the cubicle and I can smell Luca's cologne as he leans over me to reach for the shampoo. If I was in the mood, it might even be erotic being this near to each other.

'Honestly, this is why you need a man,' he mutters. 'To look after you when this kind of thing happens.'

I laugh.

'I'm perfectly able to look after myself, thanks. If I need help, I earn enough to get somebody in. Besides, apart from you, who can just pop in during your lunch hour, most husbands wouldn't be here during the day.'

'Well, you know the simple solution to that, don't you?' Luca says, as he runs the water over my pulse, getting the temperature right.

'I will not marry you, Luca,' I say, but soften the blow with a smile.

'Why not? We spend nearly every hour of every day together, anyway.'

'That's because you're my boss.'

Luca made me his CFO when he moved his father's fashion house from Milan to Lisbon after his father was murdered. The trauma and moving to a new city where we didn't know anyone else brought us closer together. We've been spending all day and every weekend since, in each other's company.

'I know we're really comfortable together, but that's not love.'

'Speak for yourself,' Luca says as he gently tilts my head back and starts playing the water over my hair.

'You don't really love me. Your affection has become a habit. You're far more interested in yourself, your clothes and the fashion house. As your wife, I'd come in a poor fourth.'

'If you were so low on my list of my priorities, I wouldn't bring you food or wash your hair,' Luca says as he turns off the tap, measures some shampoo into his hand and starts scrubbing it into my scalp. 'Are you really going to stay single forever?'

'That's the plan.'

I had been a model. I started at age twelve because my mother decided I was too beautiful to let it go to waste. She had visions of huge pay days but all I can remember of the early years were grimy changing rooms in second and third rate venues, interminable photo shoots, shows that went on too long and handsy men. So many old, disgusting men touching up every girl. If I can say one positive thing about them, it's that they worked hard at creating opportunities for themselves and their fellow creeps.

You'd think that with that kind of example, most of the women and girls on the model circuit would have developed an aversion towards men. In fact, these beautiful creatures, who should have had the upper hand, were running around currying favour. Plotting how best to snag the richest man possible. Undermining the other women who were hell bent on doing the same.

I could accept and even understand the women who were marrying for money, at least. The men in our business use and then abandon women the moment they get too old, or when the new wunderkind emerges. So why not get yourself the ultimate pay day?

It was the women with low self-esteem who thought that they had to have a man to give their existence meaning who really disturbed me. Women who thought they weren't complete human beings unless they had a husband were more the norm than the exception.

I couldn't understand them. Their constant harping on about finding a boyfriend. Their heartbreak to the point of suicidal despair when they were dumped, often for being too clingy, really freaked me out.

My mother was more on the 'every woman should have a husband' side of the spectrum, but her obsession to make me famous eventually led to my parent's divorce. Which only meant she could spend more time managing me. It was not ideal.

Fortunately, by the time I hit twenty-one and decided modelling wasn't for me, mom had found herself a man on the circuit and been sucked into managing his two gorgeous young daughters. Since she had years of experience, she was useful to him. I could exit with less drama than I'd expected and headed off to university to study economics.

4th December

CARLOTA AND THE LONG LOST CRUSH

I'm staring at the photo on my colleague's desk. It's one of those group shots taken at a conference. A crowd of people who come together over a shared interest, some superficial chats, a few deeper connections, some joint projects, lots of talks, lots of networking, litres of tea, wine and beer, and then back to the office and the daily grind.

Or, in my case, the old Lisbon aquarium. It's visited less by the public nowadays because of the flashy bigger aquarium that was built on the expo site. Our older building is attractive, small and more devoted to research.

The frame for this photo is more interesting than the picture. It's made from driftwood encrusted with tiny bleached barnacles. I reach over the piles of journals, drifts of articles and stacks of student papers and lift the frame out for a closer inspection. I start counting the number of species glued to the wood. I've reached six when I notice my face in the front row, two from the left.

'Oh!'

And, long story short, now I'm a senior manager at a fashion house.

'I've thought about it a lot,' I say while Luca massages the conditioner into my hair. 'I really like my own company. My happiest weekends are the ones I spend pottering about my house.'

'But what about emotional support?' Luca asks.

'I have wonderful friends, and even my mother. A partner isn't a guarantee of support. Sometimes they have problems of their own. Sometimes they're distracted or disinterested.'

'What about sex?'

'I don't have to be married to have sex.'

'It's easier.'

'Not really,' I say, grinning up at Luca.

He knows how easy it is for me to get a man.

'Financial support.'

'Come on,' I say with a laugh. 'Do you think we're living in the 50s? I earn more than most men.'

'True love?'

'I'll let you know if that ever happens,' I say, while Luca gives my hair a final rinse.

Then he gathers everything into a ponytail and squeezes the water out.

'You really mean to remain single your whole life, don't you?'

'I do,' I say as I towel my hair dry. 'I genuinely think I will be happiest this way. I love my life and if I have to do one of those marrying myself ceremonies to convince my friends, then I will.'

'Really?' Luca says, finally breaking into a huge grin. 'If you do, I want you to go all out and wear the most outrageous, over the top wedding dress ever seen.'

'I'll do that,' I say, and give Luca a kiss on his cheek. 'Thank you for understanding. I can promise you one thing: you will always be my best friend.'

'What?' Felicia asks.

'I'm in this photo but I don't recognise a single person here. I can't even work out when or where this was taken,' I say as I examine the tiny faces staring into the long ago camera.

Some are smiling, some solemn. I'm staring into the group, a wistful expression on my face. I follow the direction of my gaze and then I remember.

Not the time or the place, not the event or the papers, none of the colleagues, just that face. The most handsome man I've ever seen. I couldn't keep my eyes off him all through the week. But I'd been a fresh faced doctoral student then and far too shy to approach anyone.

Felicia takes the picture out of my hand and gives it the once over.

'I don't think I went to this one. I just kept it from Pedro after he retired.'

'It was for the frame, wasn't it?'

'For sure. Looks like it was something for postgrads. They all look young.'

'That might explain why I don't recognise anyone, despite the size of our field.'

In marine biology, everyone gets to know everyone.

'I wonder what happened to him,' I say, tapping that gorgeous face.

'He must have dropped out. I would have remembered him,' Felicia says with a wolfish grin.

I laugh, but I'm aching inside. How could I have avoided someone I fancied so much?

'He's probably married by now,' Felicia says. 'With kids, gained weight and balding.'

'Oh god! Don't say that!'

Felicia laughs.

'Do you think there's any way I could find out who he was?'

'Are you serious, Carlota?'

'Yeah, never more so.'

Felicia gives me a bemused look and a 'well if that's how you feel' shrug. 'The conference organisers would have his details. He probably also did a presentation, most students do at those sorts of conferences.'

'Right, so I just have to remember when and where we had that conference. Can I take the picture?'

'Help yourself,' Felicia says.

I'm already halfway back to my office, wracking my brains to remember all the conferences I attended in my doctoral days. The winter sun is shining into my office, making it pleasantly warm. Unlike Felicia, I have gone paperless, so my desk is clear aside from the computer, a stack of textbooks and a cluster of Christmas cards.

I check my online calendar. I've been putting my appointments in there for the last ten years, so it's easy enough to track down all the conferences. The problem is that I was an eager little beaver, and I attended dozens of events during my four-year doctorate.

I make a list of them all, then stare at the photo, trying to guess the time of year from the picture. I stare intently at the shrubs to either side of the pale stone stairs we posed on, trying to identify them. Trying to remember what each academic institution looked like in the vain hope I remember the stairs.

I narrow it down to autumn and most likely somewhere in Northern Europe. Then I dig through my emails. My brother told me once that it was a waste of time to delete emails. Thank god I never did and can call up all the conference bumf, programmes, registration information and attendance lists.

Next I Google every male name, at least those I don't recognise. It's astonishing and sobering to see how many of those young, dedicated and ambitious people have dropped out of the field.

By the time I get halfway down the list and have looked at the faces and public information for half the men, it's pitch black outside and getting cold in the office. I email the list to myself and head for home.

I got less done at home than expected. The following morning is filled with lectures and job related stuff, but after that I get back to my list. I've pretty much given up hope of finding the guy, but since I've come this far, I decide to finish.

And then, unexpectedly, the penultimate name on my list, Xavier Tavares is staring back at me in a hundred different poses on Google images. The man of my dreams, mostly on the deck of yachts. I giggle, astonished that I've actually found him. Even more astonished that he's Portuguese and in Lisbon. I have a colleague who's always going on about fate, which I dismiss. But this actually feels like fate.

It turns out that not only is Xavier Tavares still ruggedly good looking, but he's rich. He's used his family's money to set up a foundation to remove plastic from the sea. That explains why I couldn't find him in the world of academia. It also makes sense, because the paper he presented at that long ago conference was on micro plastics in our oceans.

I stare at his face for ages, trying to imagine making contact. What on earth can I possibly say to him? His foundation gives me a reason to contact him, but his wealth makes my already absurd fantasy even more ridiculous.

So, keeping it vague, I tell him the marine biology department of my university is interested in his work and would he mind telling me more about it. I expect I'll land up being palmed off to a junior member of staff and at that point I will accept that it was never meant to be.

The following morning, while checking my emails and telling myself that it's far too early to expect a reply, I see one. Not from the expected administrator either, from Xavier Tavares himself. What's more, he's invited me to go out on his catamaran this weekend to see their garbage collection unit! I squeal with excitement and do a little dance in my chair, waving my arms in the air.

By Saturday morning, I'm terrified as I walk into the Doca de Santo Amaro. It's the dock closest to the aquarium. I can't believe he's been so near all this time.

Why, oh why, did I think this was a good idea? I never do spontaneous things because I can't handle the fallout. But I can't back out either and I keep telling myself it's strictly business. No need for Xavier Tavares to ever suspect the real reason for my visit.

Xavier gave me a very detailed description of how to find the catamaran, but it wasn't necessary. It's one of the bigger boats in the dock and has a flag with his foundation's logo on the topmast that is snapping about in the stiff breeze.

There's also a loud argument coming from the jetty by the boat. I recognise Xavier immediately, currently shouting at a slim young woman who looks overwhelmed.

'I hate you!' she screams and runs off, tears streaming down her face.

This is not a great start.

Xavier turns, his face marred with a deep scowl. It looks as if he's going to shout something at the woman when he notices me.

'Er, hello,' I say, 'is this a bad time?'

'Dr Carlota?' he says, giving me the once over. I've dressed warmly, as instructed, with a waterproof windbreaker. It's sensible but not alluring. 'I'm sorry about that. She's my niece.'

'Oh, your niece,' I say, relieved that it wasn't an employee or worse, a far too young girlfriend.

'Come aboard. We've got rain forecast, so we're going to have to hurry if we're going to avoid it.'

'Oh yes, of course,' I say and grab the hand he holds out to help me onto the deck. This sleek, high-tech cat is a hundred years away from the old engine-powered boats I usually use for my research.

'All right, cast off,' Xavier says, waving to a crew member. Then he turns to me. 'Is this your first time on a catamaran?'

'It is,' I say, taking in the sleek lines that I expected and the luxurious cabin that I didn't. 'It's quite something.'

Xavier nods, but I can tell he's preoccupied. There's no point in trying to make conversation, but it at least gives me a chance to calm myself and get a better look at my fantasy man as he guides me to the front of the boat.

He looked older than his images, but not old, same as me: mid-thirties. Well-built, either sailing is better exercise than I assumed or he is a regular at a gym, square jawline and nice hands.

'Forgive my curiosity, but you don't look old enough to have a niece.'

I regret speaking the moment the words leave my lips.

'My sister was quite a bit older than me,' he says.

I decide against asking more. What was I even thinking talking about family to a man I've just met?

'I became my niece's legal guardian after my sister and her husband died. Most of the time we get on just fine.'

I look up at him. His gaze is fixed on the water, watching as they manoeuvre the cat out of the dock and onto the wide Tagus river. It may be my imagination, but he might just be asking for advice.

'What happened?'

'Alice is an heiress, which means a lot of men are after her for her money. I just told her... that the man she was determined to marry by Christmas is a womanising gambler.'

'Oh, the poor thing,' I say, trying to understand how I'd feel about receiving such news. 'But... why did she say she hates you?'

'Because she refused to believe me, so I told her if she marries the bastard I'll cut off her money.'

'You didn't!' I say, staring up at him in surprise.

He finally looks down at me, equally surprised.

'Why? What did I do wrong?'

'You forbade the wedding.'

'So?'

Now it's my turn to stare out across the water. It's pretty choppy as we head towards the middle of the river, angling towards the ocean. I'm trying to work out how best to explain.

'Thwarting someone's desire usually only makes them more determined to go ahead.'

'Even after what I told her about her fiancé?'

'Especially then. You've just cast yourself in the role of evil uncle. She'll probably have all sorts of romantic ideas about living happily, even in poverty. By the way, can you really cut off all her funds?'

'Until she's twenty-five, yes.'

'And how old is she now?'

'Twenty-one.'

'Ah, then she's probably convinced she can hold out until then, after which she'll shower her love with everything his heart desires.'

'You've got to be kidding,' Xavier says, looking revolted. 'So what do I do?'

'You've told her everything about this man already, right?'

'Told her, but I haven't shown her. I have evidence.'

I sigh, wondering why on earth I'm doing this but weirdly grateful I have something to talk about.

'Ultimately, she's a grownup, whether or not you think so. She has to make her own decisions and learn from her mistakes. Tell her you won't stand in the way of the wedding, but ask her to at least look at the evidence you've gathered. After that, I suppose if there's any way you can protect her fortune, you can try doing that.'

'Is that really all?'

'If you want to keep her in your life, that is the best you can do. If you don't stand by her, she'll just run full tilt into this swindler's arms.'

'If she hasn't already,' Xavier says gloomily. Then he forces a smile and takes a deep breath of the air laden with the cold salty spray the cat kicks up. 'I'm sorry to drag you into my family business when you were expecting a demonstration of our system. It is quite revolutionary. I promise you.'

I suppress my guilt and try to look interested as Xavier launches into their waste capture equipment that not only pulls out visible plastic but also filters the micro plastics. And we eventually reach the mouth of the river where the land is so far away it looks tiny and the waves have grown in size, pitching us back and forth. All this so I can be shown something that looks like a fishing net held up with high-tech buoys.

Xavier goes on at length about what everything does and it really is interesting, but the sharp wind is getting through my clothes, especially my leggings that have grown damp with spray and I'm shivering.

'Oh!' Xavier says, looking at me as if seeing me properly for the first time. 'Let's go inside. You look like you could use a coffee.'

He ushers me into the cabin, which has the feel of an upmarket lounge, and sends one of the crew for drinks.

'Thank you,' I say while I rub my numb hands together. Xavier sits down opposite me and gives me an even closer look. I pretend I don't notice.

'You know,' he says. 'I've been thinking this for a while: you look awfully familiar.'

'Do I?'

'I feel like we've met before.'

'Well... I looked you up, and you were ahead of me by a year with your doctorate, although we went to different universities.' Xavier went to a British university while I studied in Portugal. 'We probably went to quite a few of the same conferences.'

Xavier stares at me some more and, as the coffee has arrived, I stare fixedly into the inky black liquid, my hands wrapped about the mug for extra warmth.

'Oslo!' he says with a snap of his fingers that makes me jump. 'You did a talk on plankton.'

'How on earth can you remember that?'

'I just do. You were younger, and your voice was pretty shaky, but you gave one of the best talks at the conference.'

I swell with pride and glow to have been remembered. I also realise Xavier has been reserved till now. It wasn't noticeable until his enthusiasm was sparked. We end up spending over an hour talking about our favourite subject, marine biology, his work and mine.

We're so engrossed that I barely notice that I'm no longer cold, and it's only as I spot the 25th of April bridge I realise we're nearly back at the docks. I desperately want to extend our time and build a friendship with this man. He is delightful as well as good looking and intelligent. I wrack my brains for something, perhaps a joint project I can propose so that I'll meet him again.

Then the cat pulls into its berth with a bump and Xavier stands up. I follow, still searching for some way to keep seeing him. We walk in silence to the ramp that will take me off the cat and away from him and Xavier holds out his hand in farewell.

I grip it more tightly than intended.

'Thank you for a lovely afternoon. I learned so much.'

I despair at my inability to say more.

'I enjoyed myself too,' Xavier says and scratches his head. 'I um... I wonder if you'd like to meet up someday, maybe next weekend, for a meal?'

I blink at him, so astonished I can't make a sound.

'No?' he says, looking a little sad. 'I've seldom hit it off so well with anyone, Dr Carlota.'

'Me neither.'

My vocal chords have gone tight with emotion.

'So... how about Saturday?'

'I'd like that,' I say, beaming up at him.

I give him a little wave and hurry out of the dock. I'm trying hard not to skip, although my heart is bouncing like a giddy schoolgirl.

5th December

TERESA'S UNEXPECTED FLIRTATION

My name is Teresa. I sometimes forget that because most of the time I'm called Mrs Nogueira or Paula, Anna or Solange's mother by other parents and various members of academic officialdom. I'm so busy getting my girls to and from university, school, social engagements and after-school activities that I barely have time to breathe.

That's not even factoring in the girl's emotional lives, how they're getting on with their friends, fall outs, jealousies and, God help me, boyfriends. At no point in the day do I have a moment to worry about anything other than the girls, keeping the house clean and making sure we have sufficient food in the fridge. So I want to burst out laughing when the young man with the earnest blue eyes and the sun bleached hair asks me what I do for fun.

We're at the university's swanky Christmas party that's being held at The Ocean Breeze. It's the poshest hotel in Cascais and I'm feeling more than a little frumpy compared to my surroundings, all marble and crystal chandeliers, a live band playing jazzified

Christmas favourites and the svelte young students dressed in the latest, revealing fashions. Paula, my eldest, is in her second year at the university and more than able to get herself to and from parties without my help, but they have invited parents to this end-of-year bash. I'm also going to help Paula get a few things home from her dorm for the Christmas break, so I thought, why not? It's always nice to meet new people and, perhaps an interesting man. I'm already regretting it.

The students, Paula included, are clustered together, flirting, gossiping and hanging out. I watch with approval as I see her talking to one of her lecturers and an unknown tall, blond man who's too old and well-dressed to be a student but too young to be a parent. All the same, I'm pleased. I'm always telling my girls that networking is about getting to know everyone, not just people in your age group.

'So?' he prompts.

I don't get his deal. Why is this young, good-looking man chatting to me?

'I don't have time to have fun,' I say in a flat tone, intended to put him off.

'Wow!' he says, looking impressed. 'No time at all?'

'I have three teenage daughters so, no.'

It hurts to make this confession, but if anything is guaranteed to turn a guy off, it's the mention of kids. I look after myself. I like to think I look younger than my age, but I see the mental arithmetic going on in men's eyes when I mention teenage daughters. This young guy just beams at me.

'It must be tough.'

'I manage,' I say reaching for a glass of sparkling water from a tray been carried past by a waiter in s smart black and white uniform.

'But without having fun.'

'I comfort myself with the knowledge that they'll be grown up and out of the house in five or six more years.'

'That's quite a sentence,' the guy says. It feels ambiguous, with too many possible meanings. 'What about their father? Can't he help?'

Ah, the indirect 'have you got a man' question. I'm not wearing a wedding ring, which may have been why he approached me.

'I divorced my first husband, my second one died.'

Bang, bang, nails in the possible relationship coffin. He must wonder what kind of woman loses two husbands. I can tell him — someone older.

'That's bad luck,' he says with sympathy and none of the rapid distancing I expected. 'Shall I flag down one of the waiters with nibbles?'

I stare at him, dumbfounded. He's tall, well dressed, easily one of the best-looking men in the room, and in his thirties. All the other women in the hotel are looking him up and down with longing and giving me either envious or daggers looks, as if I'm the one hogging him.

'There's really no need,' I say with what I hope is a less than encouraging smile.

'My name's Marco,' he says and looks enquiringly at me.

'Teresa,' I say, wondering why he hasn't wandered off already to more interesting prey.

'I lecture at the university.'

'Ah, so you're one of the professors.' I'm guessing that his class is full of young women. 'I'm a housewife.'

'At least you don't have to add juggling a job to your workload.'

'I wish I could work. I'd like to once the girls leave home, but I'm not sure whether anyone will take me.'

'What did you study?'

'Psychology, but I doubt I could get a job in that field now. I'd have to try something else, something less skilled. Actually, I just want something to get me out of the house and give my brain a bit of stimulation.'

He smiles, actually listening, but I feel embarrassed to have said so much on a subject he's surely not interested in.

'Women returning to the workplace after a child rearing break was the topic of my doctoral thesis,' he says.

I blink at him, surprised by the turn the conversation has taken.

'What was your conclusion?'

'It's nuanced but, as you said yourself, it's difficult for anyone who takes an extended break from work to get back to the level they left at, never mind going up the pay scale.'

'And there's the loss of skills, and the way the field advances.'

'All tricky,' Marco says as the band strikes up a rendition of White Christmas.

'It's an unusual topic for a man to have studied.'

'My mother influenced me. She was also a single mom.'

I wonder whether I remind him of her. Most single moms have a frazzled look to them.

'Professor Marco?' says a dark-haired lovely with an enviable cleavage, dressed in a skin-tight sequined black sheath. She edges herself in front of me and forces me to step back. 'You look very handsome tonight.'

'Thank you, ah...'

'Pia,' she says, flashing a row of perfect white teeth. 'I'm in your Introduction to Economics class.'

She's being watched by a coven of three other girls, similarly dolled up, who look like an entourage.

'Who does she think she is?' the red head of the group says, looking me up and down.

'Must be one of the moms. She's far too old to be a student,' the one with the bleached blonde hair says.

'She's far too ugly to—'

At this point I lose interest and wander away to find myself a fizzy water, I'm driving home after all. My three daughters have far more scathing things to say and can cut me dead with the roll of an eye. Mainly because I actually care about their opinions. Queen bees and minions are irrelevant, although they are right about one thing: Prof. Marco is far too young for me. More's the pity.

I sigh and look around for Paula amongst the glittering dresses and strobing lights. I want to tell her to make her own way home. The idea of the party was more exciting than the reality and I'm too tired to start yet another conversation with a group of strangers.

'Are you leaving already?' a cool voice says at my elbow.

It's the tall, well-dressed blond who'd been speaking to Paula.

'I beg your pardon?' I say, wondering whether it's my night to be accosted by handsome men. Not that I'm complaining, mind you.

'You looked like you were leaving. As the owner of this hotel and the organiser of this event, that leaves me feeling a little...' he waves his hand and gives me a vague smile.

It's hard to read. Is he saying he'd be offended if I left?

'It is nearly midnight.'

'Exactly, far too early. You never know what might happen if you stay.'

'Some kind of witching hour magic?' I say, laughing, but it's the laugh my girls would know to be wary of.

'Ah, fighting spirit,' the blond man says, 'that must be why Marco likes you so much.'

'Professor Marco?' I glance at the group of girls that has grown around the professor. 'He's very popular. I'm sure he was just being polite to me.'

'Marco has never been interested in students, even when we were at university ourselves,' the blond says, looking me up and down even more keenly. 'My name's César, by the way.'

'Do you mean he prefers older women?' I ask in surprise.

César shrugs.

'He's never shown any interest in women at all. Which is why I agreed to be his... I believe I'd be called a wingman, or perhaps, given that it's a Christmas party, a fairy godfather?'

I laugh. This is absurd.

'Are you saying you stopped me deliberately so your friend can... what?'

'You'll have to ask him that. My role is simply to keep the competition at bay.'

'You're not doing so well on that front, are you?'

I look pointedly at Prof. Marco, just as he gives César a meaningful and rather annoyed look over the heads of all the young women giggling and fluttering their extensive eyelashes at him.

'Shall we see about that?'

César puts his arm out to herd me into the depths of the ballroom, through the milling, chatting crowd, back to his friend's side. At the same moment, several bow tie wearing waiters swoop in and start handing vouchers to the prof's admirers. It elicits squeals of delight as the entire herd stampedes towards the bar.

'Good heavens!' I say.

'Champagne vouchers,' César says and now that he's within hearing distance of Marco, he adds, 'very expensive champagne. You owe me.'

'I do,' Marco says and gives me a warm smile accompanied by, although the lighting makes it hard to tell, a blush.

'I'll continue keeping them entertained,' César says. He gives me a nod and wanders off.

'He told me he's a fairy godfather,' I say between amusement and irritation at being manoeuvred in this way.

Marco snorts his wine and then has to dab at his nose with a hanky.

'He's a bad tempered grinch. But he's right. I owe him for this. I saw him intercepting you.'

'I was about to leave.'

'That would be a shame. I'd really like to get to know you better,' Marco says as he guides me to a corner of the ball room festooned with pine and holly garlands.

'Why?' I ask, checking whether there might be some mistletoe overhead as well.

'Because you interest me. You have done from the first time I saw you, last year.'

'Last year?'

I wrack my brain trying to remember all the times I've been to the university.

'The only day that could have been was when I helped Paula move into the residence.'

'You were wearing a pair of dark blue jeans and a pale yellow jumper.'

'Good lord, you even remember that?'

'And I've asked your daughter about you. She pretty much gave me her blessing for... getting to know you.'

'Oh,' I say, staring at this man as if he's lost his mind.

He's very handsome, much more than my previous husbands, and a lot younger too. At least ten years younger than me.

'This is not a good idea.'

'Why? Because it doesn't conform to societal norms? Isn't that a bit old-fashioned? Especially coming from you.'

'What's that supposed to mean?'

'Paula told me that your youngest daughter was your second husband's child, but you took her in after he died.'

'Well... I mean, I couldn't just abandon her.'

'I know this will sound very forward of me, but we live in a modern world where blended families aren't uncommon, so perhaps you could consider adding me into the mix?'

'I am not marrying for a third time,' I say firmly.

Marco laughs.

'I wasn't thinking that far... yet. But I'm hoping that you'll at least go out with me if I invite you to dinner.'

If it wasn't for the fact that I'd been sticking to soda water all night, I would have blamed inebriation for my reply.

'Why not?' I say nonchalantly. 'It's nearly Christmas after all.'

6th December

ELENA'S IMPOSITION

I'm a bitch and I know it. An insecure bitch just craving attention, or so my shrink says. And rich. Really, really rich. I could be richer too if it weren't for the patriarchy. My half-brother, the eldest admittedly, is about to be made the CEO of the company. This really pisses me off.

Until a year ago, he was only the Director of the perfume house. The most prestigious branch of the Zeller Group. I was the Marketing Director, still am.

Then Armando, the half-brother, went and found himself a wife. An old family foe, no less, and any day now she's going to have a baby. They already know it's a boy. Dad couldn't be more ecstatic. Not only is the eldest son going to take over the family firm, but he's even got his successor lined up.

On top of that, Armando has foisted his choice of personal assistant on me. I mean, the cheek of the man and he had the nerve to tell me it's my fault. Can I help it if everyone around me is incompetent? I know old fogeys are always complaining about useless young people, but in this one instance, they're absolutely right. None of my previous PAs were worth a damn.

Anyway, this PA... I'm going to set a new record with him. He may be a man, all the others have been women, but he'll be leaving in tears before the end of the day just the same.

There's a tap at the door. Do I detect hesitancy?

'Come!' I say at my imperious best.

The new PA's not quite what I expected. I thought Armando would send an intimidating bruiser. Instead, this man is only slightly taller than me if I'm wearing flats, but we're exactly eye to eye in my heels. He's wearing a plain grey off-the-peg suit, slightly scuffed black shoes, white shirt, slim black tie, glasses, and has mid-brown hair. He looks unnaturally pale, but that's the only thing that tells me he's frightened.

'Doctor Elena?' he says and holds out his hand.

I give it a brief shake.

'And you are?'

'Jaime Lemos, your new PA? HR should have told you I was coming?'

HR huh, so that's how they're going to play it, is it?

Jaime looks past me at my office. It's very girly, deliberately so.

A beautiful, spindly gold desk stands beside a French window that looks out onto the main avenue of Lisbon. The leafless trees outside are screened by gossamer curtains. Opposite is a chaise dotted with cushions and a few lacy throws, and I've lined our full range of beautiful perfume bottles up on my desk.

Since it's nearly Christmas, there's also gold and green tinsel wound around the room. It looks more like a boudoir than an office, as Dad never fails to point out.

'Don't worry, your desk is in the boring office you just came through,' I say. 'Although today I'll need you here. I have a busy day, so we may as well start. You've already worked in the company for five years, correct?'

'That's right,' Jaime says and flicks on his tablet. 'I have your diary for the day. You're due to see the company president in half an hour. I've ordered a coffee, which should arrive shortly.'

As he speaks, there's another tap at the door and a junior member of staff pushes in a trolley with my coffee and a selection of pastel-coloured macarons.

'I don't eat sweets, they're bad for my blood sugar,' I snap.

Bad for my figure, really, but I'll never admit to that. I drink the double espresso in a single gulp and slam the cup back on the trolley the hapless junior is still manoeuvring out of the office.

'Let's get one thing straight,' I say, glaring at Jaime. 'I consider you a spy sent by my brother. I don't trust you as far as I can throw you. Although that may be further than I'd been expecting.'

'I understand,' Jaime says and actually manages not to flinch, which kind of impresses me. 'My only allegiance will be to you, however.'

I look at him like he's lost his marbles. Allegiance? No PA has ever had the nerve to say anything like that before.

'Do you have the report for my father?' I say, holding out a hand.

'I've emailed it to you and have this paper copy for him,' he says, holding out a black folder edged with gold.

I make sure all my folders are in this same style, so Dad, current company president and CEO, is fully aware of who is sending him the best work. I'm surprised Jaime knows this, though. It was one thing I was going to trip him up on.

'I'll need you to minute the meeting,' I say while skimming the marketing report.

I commissioned the report and told the researchers what I wanted in it. Their results don't come as a surprise. I may look like a socialite in the latest fashion and with my hair in a perfect high ponytail, but nobody works harder than me.

Jaime follows at a discreet distance as I head for the president's office. Dad actually looks impressed by him, unlike my previous PAs who all got an eye roll. Dad's PA, selected by my mother, is a middle-aged woman who wouldn't look out of place on the Russian shot put team. She's damn good at her job, though, which is why she's been his PA for nearly twenty years now.

I wonder what it would be like to have a PA for so long. Few of mine have lasted more than six months.

After the meeting with Dad I have a string more: market researchers, social media influencers and a briefing from the product development team which involves a visit to our factory in the industrial park. Jaime, surprisingly, is not only keeping up, but on the ball. I haven't had a single chance to bawl him out yet. Every document is in order, every meeting meticulously planned and minuted. He even hands me a salad and Diet Coke from a cool bag while we ride back to the office.

'You have been well briefed,' I say as I ease open the lid on my lunch. 'Did my brother tell you what to do?'

'Do you mean Dr Armando Zeller, ma'am?'

'Who else would I mean?'

My younger brother, Eddy, recently left the firm to spend his days as a professional surfer. It nearly gave Dad an aneurysm.

'I haven't actually met Dr Armando,' Jaime says in an apologetic tone. 'I mean, I've seen him at meetings and events, but we've never spoken.'

'So how come he recommended you to HR?'

This sounds suspicious, although Armando is well known for avoiding people. He has a fantastic sense of smell, which is what makes him our top perfumer, but he's not keen on smelling the rest of stinking humanity from whom he keeps his distance. He doesn't even shake hands.

'As far as I understand,' Jaime says, 'HR sent him a shortlist of candidates. I have no idea why I was the one he selected.'

'Odd,' I mutter and stab half a cherry tomato with my fork and stare at it as if it's got the answers.

Several meetings later and I'm back at my desk going over our daily marketing reports of media coverage and analysis of our newest advert's performance. It's been a long day and I have a headache coming on, so I'm massaging my temple with my index finger.

An elegant pink and gold tea cup filled with gently steaming water and a slice of lemon is slipped into my line of sight, along with a box of painkillers. I look up, intent on slapping Jaime down, certain he's standing there waiting for praise, but he's actually on his way out.

'What are you still doing here? I thought I told you to go home.'

'Not before the boss,' Jaime says as he half turns towards me and gives a slight nod. 'Just buzz me if you need anything else.'

He would have got an earful if he had gone home, so he's just sidestepped another of my traps.

'The HR director… see if she's still around. Tell her I want a word.'

'Yes, ma'am,' Jaime says, keeping his face neutral, but there's a twitch.

Is he wondering whether he's about to be fired? Whatever. At least the HR director is still around and comes up to see me immediately.

'Rosa,' I say, giving her a smile even though we're not on good terms. 'Please sit down.'

'What can I help you with, Elena?' she asks perching on the edge of my chaise.

She's complained about the look of my office before. Apparently it's unprofessional. I told her to judge me on results. She said staff retention is also a part of the package where I fall woefully short and, what's more, people skills should be used in-house as well as out.

Everyone outside the company loves me. I make sure of that. It's my job.

'Tell me, Rosa,' I said as I take a sip of lemon tea, 'what criteria you and Armando used to select Jaime Lemos for the post of PA?'

'The same criteria I always use when selecting PAs,' Rosa says, reflecting my insincere smile. 'And if I might add, it was the president who ordered Dr Armando to be involved in the selection and he was… light touch.'

'What do you mean by light touch?'

'Once we had interviewed the final six candidates, I sent Dr Armando the CVs, interview notes and scoring sheets and he made the decision on who to recruit from that.'

'Did he take your first choice?'

'I maintain impartiality by always offering the post to the highest scorer. Dr Armando chose the candidate that came in third.'

'Was he the highest scoring man?'

I ask because that would make sense even though I haven't particularly thought of Armando as sexist up till now. All sorts of other things, but not that.

'There was another male candidate that came second.'

'So why Jaime?'

'Dr Armando said he shows resilience.'

'Resilience?'

'I believe his primary criteria was to pick somebody who would hold on to the job no matter what,' Rosa says, still with that insincere smile. 'Now, if you'll excuse me, I have to pick my daughter up from day care.'

I wave her away and go back to work. But I can't focus and a couple of hours later I'm reaching for the intercom button.

'Jaime!' I say, 'Are you still there?'

'Yes, ma'am.'

'Come and see me.'

I lean back, running through what I remember of Jaime's CV. It's distinctly average. Average school, average grades, a marketing degree from an average university, and five years working for two mid-level underperforming managers at Zeller.

He was aiming high when he applied to work for me. Then again, Rosa has told me that my reputation is so bad, good PAs never apply.

Jaime steps into the room. He looks tense.

'What can I do for you, Dr Elena?'

'Sit,' I say, waving at the chaise. 'Tell me about yourself.'

'Do you want my qualifications?'

He's sitting ramrod straight, feet together, the edge of his tablet resting on his knees, using it like a shield.

'My brother apparently thinks you're resilient. What would give him that impression?'

Jaime looks taken aback and tilts his head to think, a slight crease forming between his brows.

'My first boss at Zeller was a bully and incompetent, but I stuck it out and he got fired before I did. The second boss was very good at claiming other's work as his own, but I stayed on while I looked for another position when many of my colleagues just quit.'

I'm getting the picture.

'You can't afford to quit, can you?'

'Not really,' Jaime says and hands me a printout of an email. 'You asked if I'd met Dr Armando. As I said, I haven't, but he did send me this yesterday.'

It's in my brother's typically brief style.

Congratulations on your promotion.

Dr Elena is an impatient perfectionist who works exceptionally long hours. She will expect a lot of you. If you are on the ball and give her your loyalty, you will both benefit from the partnership.

Good luck.

'Bloody Armando!'

It's so typical of him. I've been a bitch to him my whole life, at home and at work. I was ready to fight him to the death to get my hands on the company and he ignores me. Or worse, sends that kind of infuriating email.

'Are you in the habit of showing people emails from senior staff?' I ask and give Jaime my steeliest stare.

'This is my first and last time, ma'am. I just didn't want to keep it from you, as you asked about Dr Armando earlier.'

'Is this you being loyal?'

'I am committed to you and the company.'

'But you put me first?'

'If that is what you wish me to do.'

This man is totally mad, I think, while staring into large brown puppy dog eyes. Who in their right mind would be this devoted to a boss, especially a boss like me?

Then again, I worked him hard today, and he survived. He looks tired but not broken. None of my other PAs would still be with me in the office with the clock ticking towards 10pm. Most would already have gone home — permanently.

'Alright, you can stay,' I say and waggle a finger at him. 'But I am going to work you till you're sweating blood and crying tears of exhaustion.'

'I look forward to it, ma'am.'

'Okay,' I say as I leap to my feet and sling my Chanel jacket over my shoulders, 'I'm going home. I'll see you tomorrow.'

'See you tomorrow,' Jaime says, and I let him have his small smile of triumph.

This man is not bad even if he is shorter than any man I've dated before. Where did that thought come from? Then I laugh. Maybe I've found somebody who'll be more than a PA one day.

7th December

FÁTIMA AND THE POWER OF FLOWERS

I'm standing at the counter of my favourite café getting my early shot of caffeine. It's a deliciously fragrant duplo that's guaranteed to blast away any lingering sleepiness. I knock it back and head for the till, my money already in hand.

I'm a regular, but José, the café owner, usually only has time to take my money with a grunted, 'Good morning,' before he's off to serve the next customer.

They're nearly two deep at the bar this morning. Unexpectedly, he hands me a slip of paper along with my change.

'What's this?'

He gives me a grin and a shrug and he's off. I'm exasperated, but shove it in my pocket while also trying to get my change into my purse, and my purse back into the bag, as I shuffle towards the exit. I sling my bag over my shoulder as I step out into the bright December sun. It's such a relief after the gloom of the November rains, but chilly and a bit too bright. So I wrap my wonderful chunky cardigan more tightly about myself and knot the belt, then I put on my enormous sunglasses. They are, my friends tell me, very chic and the same deep red as my hair.

It's only then that I fish out the slip of paper. It's a nice textured paper of the sort used by artists. On it is a pretty, minimalist drawing of a daisy. There's a flair to this simple drawing. Whoever created it has talent. It doesn't thrill me though.

I work at a publishing house. I'm the chief editor for the on-line bandas desenhadas, BDs for short, comics for our English-speaking clients. Over the years, aside from being swamped by a tidal wave of manuscripts and art from wannabe artists and BD authors, I have also had all sorts of cunning and far out approaches made to get my attention. Still, the art is nice, so it gets pinned to the corkboard in my office rather than going in the bin.

The next day, in the similarly busy cafe, I get a second image. This time it's an elegant stem of bluebells. The day after a spiky dandelion head, some seeds spinning off in an invisible wind.

This time the café is quiet, so I say, 'José, I'm not letting you see another customer until you tell me who is giving you these pictures.'

I use the tone of voice I've perfected to kick my writers into gear when they complain about writer's block. Nobody has dared to stand up against me then. José doesn't even put up a fight.

'I don't know who he is. But he usually arrives before you, sits at a table, has a coffee and a croissant and off he goes.'

'So he's a regular?'

'Since about a month or two ago.'

That could mean he's arrived relatively recently but now lives or works nearby.

'What does he look like?'

José shrugs.

'Young, tall, dark hair, always dressed in black.'

'When you say young...'

'About your age, early thirties.'

'Will you point him out to me tomorrow?'

'If I have a chance.'

I make sure José doesn't forget by glaring at him meaningfully the next morning, and he tilts his chin towards a table by the café window. I spin around, whack a fellow customer with my bag and his coffee flies out of his hand, bounces on the counter, splashing liquid everywhere, then tumbles onto the floor, shattering.

I'm so busy apologising to both the customer and José that the man is gone by the time I've smoothed everything over. He left me another drawing, though, this time of a purple and yellow pansy.

I caught enough to identify the man the following morning. He's sitting in the same spot. José left out the fact that he's handsome, outrageously so. I'm sure he has hundreds of women making moves on him.

This time I take my coffee and, making sure I do nothing sudden, weave my way through the early morning throng towards his table. He looks up, as if he's searching somebody out and our eyes meet.

I smile and raise my hand in greeting. He gives a start then makes a run for the door, leaving a half-eaten croissant, his money and a picture of a twining stem of honeysuckle on the little round metal table.

I pocket the picture. It was surely meant for me anyway and head for the office where I pin the flower pictures in a row marching across the board.

The next day, the man doesn't appear. I wonder whether I've scared him off, or whether he doesn't come to the cafe on the weekend. He has more than piqued my curiosity. Especially if it had been a ploy to get me to commission him. He should have stayed to talk, not bolted.

So today I get to the café way earlier than usual, down my essential pick-me-up, and head back outside where I lurk behind the wheelie bins. An awful choice, as the stink is overwhelming. But my suffering pays off. The man comes in looking furtive and probably also earlier than usual. Seems he's trying to avoid me.

He leaves looking... disappointed? I like to think it's that, anyway. Maybe he's sorry he missed me. He walks along for two blocks, crosses the road and heads up the hill for another three. It's a good thing I told the office I was going to be out meeting writers this morning.

Finally he stops at a florist, rolls up the shutters, unlocks the front door, ties on a green and white striped apron and starts to carry potted plants and large tubs of cut flowers, leaves and gold and silver sprayed ornamental branches outside. So he's a florist. Florêncio, Flowers of the Highest Quality, is written in a pretty blue font on the green board above the shop. I wonder if that's his name. It would be the height of nominative determination if it was. It suits him. He is a very handsome flower.

I back track to the café and José hands me a picture of an upright stem of lavender. The next day, it's the sweetest bunch of tiny blue forget-me-nots.

'Does he ever say anything to you about these?' I ask José.

'Not a word, but he's got a stutter, and seems to be very shy.'

Ah, now things are making sense. I know an awful lot of artists. Many of them are perfectly ordinary, well-balanced types. But the other half are some of the oddest oddballs you could ever hope to meet.

One of whom I'm supposed to be meeting this morning, so I hurry to the office clutching my latest offering. My current theory is that I've got myself an artist who is too shy for the direct approach. But if he yearns to become a BD artist, he's ultimately going to have to screw up his courage and speak to me. I'm all for nurturing talent, but even I have limits.

Maria Jesus is already in my office when I arrive. She's a synesthete who sees words and sounds in colour and tastes, and is the creator of our top selling BD: Magic Kingdom. She's also notoriously introverted and the best I've ever been able to do is insist on an annual end-of-year meeting at the office. The rest of the time, I have to go and see her.

She's a small woman who always dresses in black when she ventures out into the world, although she has a princess-y dress style at home. At the moment, all I can see is her back with her floppy black hat tilted all the way up as she examines the pictures on the board. She focuses on the board to block out the cacophony of stimulation that comes from a busy office.

'Good morning, Jesus,' I say, heading for my desk to offload my bag.

'Morning,' she says, giving me her usual timid smile. 'I see you've got an admirer.'

'What are you talking about? I'm far too busy to pick up a boyfriend and I'd notice if I did.'

'Oh, those flower pictures,' Jesus says, pointing back at the board.

'Those flowers?' I say blankly and lay the latest one on the desk.

Jesus turns back to the board and puts her finger on the first image.

'Daisy — she loves me, she loves me not. Bluebell — pushing a person towards love. Dandelion — how long must I wait? Pansy — I love you. Honeysuckle — I love you a lot. Lavender — I'm sorry. Forget-me-not — well, that one's obvious.'

She turns back with a smile and a shrug, but I'm thunderstruck.

'Are you telling me I'm being stalked by some love struck stranger who's leaving me a code in flowers?'

'It was very popular in Victorian times,' Jesus says. 'Although I'm more worried about the stalking?'

'Well... I suppose it's just been passing notes at the café, aside from that he hasn't made an approach.'

'He's probably just shy,' Jesus says.

We have other things we need to discuss, so we switch to her work. I can barely concentrate, and the rest of the morning is no better. These kinds of things are best dealt with immediately. So as the clock gets to lunchtime, I head for the florist.

Fortunately, he doesn't close for lunch. But now that I've arrived, after having planned a couple of cutting opening lines, I hover at the door, taking in the plants. I also notice a revolving display filled with hand painted Christmas cards featuring gorgeous illustrations of frosted plants. I have an unreasonable moment of jealousy. How dare he sell something he made for me? Then I laugh. I'm being absurd.

'Can I help you?' comes from the dim interior of the shop.

My handsome note passer steps out, blinking into the light, realises it's me and takes a step back.

'No!' I say, holding up my hand. 'Stop running away.'

He freezes on the spot.

'Have you been sending me love notes?'

'I'm s.s.sorry,' he mutters. 'I couldn't w.w.work up the courage to speak to you. You're very... very...'

'Forceful, bold, larger than life?'

'Yes,' he says, looking relieved that I get it but also dismayed.

'Is your name Florêncio?'

He nods and flushes as red as the bunches of roses behind him.

'Do you know I edit BDs?'

'You do what?'

Well, that clears up one of my questions.

'I also work with a lot of shy introverts and I find it tiring.'

'I see,' he says and his gaze drops to the shiny white cobbles of the pavement and I note his deep brown, almost black, eyes and his long eyelashes.

'I'm not entirely opposed to giving you a chance, though.'

'You aren't?' he says, looking back up with an endearing spark of puppy-like hope.

'I might be persuaded over lunch. No need to make it fancy.'

He looks at me, surprised and a bit confused.

'Now?'

'Can you think of a better time?'

'Not at all, j.j.just let me close the shop,' Florêncio says as he whips off his apron.

I watch as he closes the shop and puts a note up that he's gone to lunch. I like that he's quick to figure things out and to act. Maybe this flower romance has a chance after all.

8th December

VANESSA AND THE HUMUNGOUS BILL

Three hundred and fifty-two euros and twenty-three cents. I stare at the bill, trying to make sense of it, but the numbers blur on the paper in my quivering hand. How did I even get to this point?

It started a week ago when my... I can hardly call him my boyfriend anymore, suggested that as it was coming up to our three-year anniversary, and my birthday, we should go all out and have a fancy celebration.

I'm the one that worries about money in our relationship. Neither of us earns very much. I work at a laundromat. Urbino's an odd-jobs man come cleaner at one of those dingy little hotels in the less trendy part of Lisbon.

But he tells me he's been saving up all year for this. It surprises me, money doesn't stay in Urbino's pockets for very long.

The clincher, though, is when he says, 'Come on, your birthday is so near Christmas nobody ever makes much of it. Just this once, let's do something special.'

So I let him talk me into going to the Michelin starred restaurant on the top floor of the Ocean Breeze Hotel. I'm flattered that he thinks so much about me, but the rest makes me nervous. I don't even have the right clothes for this kind of place. It's all soft lighting, linen tablecloths, silver cutlery of multiple different knives and forks, gold-rimmed plates, candles and a row of five wine glasses.

A pianist tinkles away as they lead us to our table, booked six months in advance by Urbino, also out of character. I've never known him to plan for anything.

I'm wearing my mother's black dress, hand made but, as she always said, in a classical style that will never go out of fashion. It looks a bit like a Chanel. I dipped into my meagre savings to buy a nice pair of matching black shoes and got a haircut.

I was feeling confident until I walked into the restaurant. Then all the glittering women dripping expensive jewellery, flashing perfectly manicured and painted fingernails and immaculate make-up, leave me feeling frumpy. I hide my hands, red and rough from using detergents all day, behind my back.

The waiter is professional and pulls my chair out for me like he would for any of those stately, magazine-cover-worthy women. Urbino is grinning from ear to ear.

'Look at that view,' he says waving at the Cascais bay, twinkling with lights.

'It's beautiful,' I say, and now that we're seated, it feels almost like we're in our own little world.

Not quite. I'm distracted by an extraordinary-looking man. He's sitting in my line of sight, so it's difficult not to look at him. He's the tallest man I've ever seen. Even sitting down, he's as tall as the staff and customers that stroll past him. He's also got a shock of coppery red hair that glows in the candlelight.

He's taken off his suit jacket and his white shirt is tight around bulging muscles. He doesn't have an ounce of fat, yet he had to squeeze into his chair. But he looks at ease, even though he's by himself.

Throughout our expensive dinner, he's there, happily working his way through a vast selection of plates that, having looked at the menu, I reckon must add up to a cool thousand euros.

I'm more cautious, even though Urbino encourages me to splurge. He goes for the lobster. The prices are too scary for me to really enjoy anything and I've ordered all the cheapest dishes on the menu.

After dessert and coffee, the priciest coffee in all of Portugal, Urbino says he needs to use the bathroom and wanders off.

He stays away so long that the restaurant is starting to empty. Only the red-headed man and a few couples are still dotted about. I keep making eye contact with the big man, which is embarrassing.

Now seriously worried, I call Urbino's mobile. It goes to voicemail, so I ask our waiter if he can check the bathrooms. He comes back to say there is nobody there. I call Urbino again. Voicemail again.

That's when the waiter brings me the bill. That's why I'm staring at it, wondering what I can do. I don't even own a credit card and my debit card will be rejected for insufficient funds.

For a crazy moment, I wonder whether they'll accept my offer to wash dishes. Does that ever work?

'Are you ready to pay, madam?' the waiter asks, sidling up to me, card machine in hand.

'Just give me a moment,' I say, but I barely register him.

I'm feeling dizzy, sick, shaken to my core. It isn't the bill, it's what Urbino did. It's how much planning this must have taken. He booked the restaurant six months ago, but he clearly had no intention of paying for this meal. It's just like him to want to splurge on something he could never afford. But why not do it on his own? Why drag me into it?

I can think of only one reason. He wanted to leave me but in his cowardly way, he couldn't just say so. He found a devastating way to do it, though. I never want to see him again.

I contemplate making a run for it too, but I can't. I can't stoop to his level. A tear slips from my eye and trails down to my chin before dropping onto my dress. I turn to face the window so the remaining guests can't see me. The view that had been twinkly and romantic before just seems chilly now. A wintery wind rocking the boats in the harbour.

'Here,' says an unexpected, deep voice, and a hanky appears.

'Thank you,' I mutter and dab at my eyes, trying to stem the tide.

I'm even more embarrassed now. It takes a while before I muster up the courage to look around. I'm astonished to find the red-headed giant grinning at me.

'My date didn't even turn up,' he says.

'I'm sorry.'

'I wasn't really looking forward to meeting her.'

That sounds weird, but I've got bigger problems. The waiter is approaching. It feels like doom, and even worse, I'm going to have to confess, in front of this stranger, that I don't have the money.

The waiter picks up the leather folder, tucks the bill back into it, says, 'All paid, thank you, madam,' gives the red-headed man a regal nod, and wanders off.

I stare at the waiter's retreating back in astonishment, then turn to the redhead.

'I didn't pay.'

'It's okay, I did. It wasn't hard to figure out what happened.'

'But... I don't know you,' I say and wonder how a giant like this can suddenly look angelic.

Then I start to panic. A total stranger, one who has been stood up, no less, paying such an enormous bill. He must want something in return.

'If you give me your name and bank details, I'll pay you back.'

I have to draw a line. Make sure he can't demand anything else.

'There's really no need,' he says.

'No, I insist. It's very kind of you, but I can't take money from a stranger.'

'Alright, if that's what you'd prefer,' he says, takes out his phone and waves it meaningfully at mine.

I give him my number and get a text back, with the name Ragno Oldenbourg.

'That's an unusual name.'

'Have you never heard of it?'

'Why would I have?'

Ragno laughs.

'You can't imagine what a pleasure it is to meet somebody who doesn't know who I am.'

I look him over again. He's even bigger up close, but also younger than I first thought. His face is boyish and his eyes sparkle like the world is filled with wonder. You'd think someone so distinctive would stick in my memory.

'Are you a celebrity? Maybe a famous sportsman?'

'Nope,' he says, giving me a goofy grin. 'So what's your name?'

'Oh, of course, I should have said, I'm Vanessa Enes.'

'Nice to meet you, Vanessa. And since you are determined to repay me, I can think of other ways that don't involve money.'

My heart sinks. Of course, I can think of ways too.

'Have a meal with me,' Ragno says.

It wasn't what I expected.

'I beg your pardon?'

'No,' Ragno says, looking thoughtful. 'Your bill was three hundred and something, wasn't it? I think it will have to be three meals, and one coffee break.'

'You want me to buy you three meals?' I'm doing the calculations. At one meal a month, I can just about afford it. 'Can you wait until January for the first one?'

'No, not buy me a meal. Be my date.'

'Why would you want that?' I ask, my suspicion deepening.

'Because you're cute and because my really rich family keeps trying to set me up with other really rich families. Although, as you can see from tonight, some of them aren't keen either.'

The mention of wealth tickles my memory. I have a feeling the Oldenbourgs have something to do with banking.

'Also,' Ragno carries on, 'My eldest brother, Bernardo, is getting married for the second time and I'm getting hell from my mother for never marrying. If you come to the wedding with me, I'll call that the meal plus the coffee date.'

'I can't go with you to a wedding! I hardly know you.'

'There's plenty of time. The wedding's on the 20th.'

'The 20th of what?' I ask before I realise that I'm being dragged along by this man's infectious enthusiasm instead of just giving him a straight no.

'December,' Ragno says cheerfully.

'That's hardly any time at all.'

'Well, we've made a start, haven't we? One more meal before the wedding and we'll be like old friends.'

'But... I mean, I work at a laundromat. How can I possibly go to a wedding filled with wealthy, well-educated people?'

'Not a problem,' Ragno says with an airy wave of one gigantic hand. 'Most of the women I've dated don't work at all. My mother will most likely admire your work ethic.'

I have my doubts but I'm warming to this crazy giant.

'What harm would it do?' Ragno says in an encouraging tone. 'Why not join me for a meal in a week's time? If that goes well, we can talk about the rest.'

'Okay,' I say, swept along by his charm and enthusiasm.

I feel like I've stepped out of my constrained little world with the dastardly Urbino and into a world suddenly filled with Ragno-shaped possibilities.

9th December

FERNANDO MAKES A HASH OF THINGS

Everything is ready. Margarida's shop is always closed on Mondays, and I've taken the day off work. I've been planning this for weeks. I had a false start a month ago when I did all the prep but had a last-minute case go to court and I had to cancel everything. I've never felt more thwarted.

Today, everything will be perfect. I arrive at Margarida's shop bang on time. She has a little knickknacks store filled with homemade beeswax candles and embroidered items, from baby clothes to dishcloths. When she's not seeing to customers Margarida sits in a corner of her shop embroidering and creating new designs. I love sitting with her while she works.

It isn't always comfortable and I still find myself ducking if Diana, Margarida's best friend, neighbour and my ex comes past.

I toot my horn, and nothing happens. I'd expected Margarida to come flying down the stairs to fling herself into my arms. I count to ten and toot again. Still nothing. How can this be?

I park the car as a queue of cars is forming behind me in the lane which is so narrow only a single car can go down it at a time. It takes me fifteen minutes to find a spot and I'm stress sweating now.

I walk back to Margarida's and ring the bell. No answer. So I call her.

'Fernando, where are you?' she asks, and she sounds anxious.

'What do you mean? I'm at your house. Hurry and come down.'

'Come down? I thought we were meeting at the castle?'

I swear under my breath. I love Margarida to death, but she can be exasperatingly unfocused at times.

'No, I said I'd pick you up at home.'

Silence on the line.

Then, 'No, you said we'd meet at the Moorish castle. Hurry and come here. I'm getting cold.'

I'm about to argue, to make it clear she's misunderstood, again. But no, not today.

'Okay, I'm on my way. Where exactly are you?'

'At the entrance.'

She sounds annoyed, which makes me angry. I'm also in a hurry and curse as a never-ending stream of cars prevents me from getting out of my tight parking space. Finally, somebody decides they want the spot and stops. I pull out at speed and get about 200 meters when I hit a traffic jam. I bang my fist on the horn even though I know it won't make any difference. It doesn't even make me feel better. Margarida is outside in the biting December wind waiting for me and getting crosser with every passing minute.

I wind my way slowly up the narrow Sintra lane, accepting that I just have to sit behind this line of cars and tuc-tucs ferrying tourists to one of the most popular ruins in the villa.

'Sorry I'm late, I'm late,' I say as I hurry to Margarida who's glaring at me, her arms wrapped tight about her puffer jacket.

I hug her, banging the big black bag I'm carrying against her back.

'Ouch,' Margarida says and pushes me away.

She's looking grumpy.

'I'm a local, Fernando. I don't need to see this place again, especially not on such a chilly day.'

'It will be worth it,' I say as I grab one of her warm, woolly-gloved hands and pull her along.

We can sail past the queue because I bought tickets online. I plotted out the route last month and know exactly where we're going. I lead Margarida, who's dragging her feet, to a secluded corner with a magnificent view out over the gigantic boulders, across the forest, all the way to the deep blue sea.

'Isn't this fantastic?' I ask and turn Margarida around to look.

'It is,' she says, and her face softens.

'You keep looking this way. I've got something to set up.'

'What?'

'It's a surprise, so don't look.'

I put the black bag down and start unpacking. First a strip of red carpet, then an entire bag of red paper rose petals that start blowing away the moment I scatter them on the ground. I hadn't counted on the strength of the wind. After corralling them into a corner, I take out the bag of candles. I lay them out in the shape of a heart and out comes the lighter. It's bloody impossible to get them lit. I barely light one flame when the wind extinguishes it.

'What are you doing?' Margarida asks, and she's shivering despite her warm clothes.

'I'm almost ready, just a second more.'

I've finally managed to get three flames to remain lit when a powerful gust lifts my paper petals and flings them into my candles. Those bastard things stay lit long enough to set the petals alight.

'Damn it to hell!' I bellow, and start stamping out the mini blaze.

Margarida swings around.

'Fernando, what's going on?'

'That's what I want to know too,' says the masculine voice of one of the security guards.

'What?' I say.

'No fires allowed. This is a heritage site.'

'Oh, sorry,' I say and rub the remaining ashes into the smoke-stained carpet with my foot.

'Take the carpet away too,' the guard says, giving me an unimpressed up and down look before he leaves.

'What is going on?' Margarida says, looking quite lost. 'This isn't like you.'

I know that all too well.

'I was trying to be romantic,' I mutter.

Should I give up? The mood hasn't been great from the start and I feel worse now since Margarida hasn't even guessed what I'm up to. Are we so far out of sync?

No, today has to be the day.

I whip out the little blue velvet box from my pocket and go down on one knee, ignoring the family of tourists who've slowed down to watch.

'Margarida, will you do the honour of marrying me?'

'What?' Margarida whispers.

This shocked reaction was not what I was expecting.

'Will you marry me?'

'No, Fernando, no. How could I?'

I'm stunned. I get up off the ground and brush my knee clean.

'Why not? Don't you love me?'

'I do. Of course I do, but how can we? Diana...' Margarida says in a stricken voice.

She's always felt guilty over our relationship.

'But I broke up with Diana long before we got together. Didn't I?' I say, wiping my brow.

Could this day get any worse?

'Yes.'

'And she's happily married to a guy I even tried to get her back from.'

'True.'

'Without success, even though you tried your best to help me.'

'Yes.'

'And they're about to have a kid.'

'I know,' Margarida says, but her head is bowed and she's avoiding eye contact.

'Are you afraid you are my second best?'

'I can't help but feel guilty.'

'Don't,' I say and fold her in my arms. 'I may have botched this proposal but please believe me about this. Honestly, Margarida, Diana and I weren't right for each other. She's much happier with Armando, and I'm much happier with you.'

'And I love you,' Margarida says into my chest.

'Will you feel better if I phone Diana and get her permission?' I say, fishing in my pocket.

'Don't do that,' Margarida squeaks.

'So, will you marry me then?'

Margarida looks up, her makeup smudged with tears that somehow make her look even more endearing.

'Yes, I will marry you,' she says. 'Sorry for being so foolish.'

I want to whoop for joy and fist pump the air.

Instead, I wrap Margarida in a tight embrace and say, 'I will always try my best to make you happy. Now let's get off this chilly mountain top and have a hot mulled wine somewhere fancy.'

10th December

DOROTEIA AND THE SURGEON

I'm sitting at my computer, late into the night trying to finish a novel with a looming deadline and cowering while Mother Nature lets loose. Lighting jabs through the air overlaid by thunder which is literally shaking the house. The pine trees are thrashing about so violently I'm worried they're going to either blow over and crush the house or something big is going to snap and fly through my window. If not a branch then the squalls of rain clattering like stones against the glass might finish them.

I've long since unplugged the laptop. The last thing I need is a power surge to fry my decades of precious work. It's backed up in the cloud, I'm not so irresponsible. I'm just not sure I know how to get it off the cloud.

I jump at the bang of a too-close-for-comfort lightning strike and the lights trip, plunging me into blackness until my eyes readjust to the pale illumination from my computer screen. I'm shaking.

I peer out of the window, trying to see whether I'm the only one to have lost power. There are no lights coming from my sparsely sprinkled neighbours up the hill. I'm nearer the bottom and a small stream forms the border of my garden.

While I'm rubbing at the continuously misting glass to double check, the bright beams from a car draw my attention. It's going too fast, especially in this weather. Then it veers and the high beams pierce the darkness dazzling me. That isn't possible, the road runs parallel, lights never shine into my kitchen. Then it's gone but I can hear a long loud car horn.

I look back out the window and down to the only source of light, a car, bonnet first in my little stream.

'Shit!' I say and reach for my phone to call 999.

I don't have a signal. Whatever knocked out the power has apparently also done for the phone tower. I'm not the brave type, I just write about them. My hero wouldn't hesitate. He'd be out the door in a flash and save whoever is in the car. I feel ashamed that I'm so terrified I'm frozen to the spot.

But somebody is out there, in the stream. It might be narrow enough to jump across on a normal day but it turns into a raging torrent when it rains. I have to do something.

I send a text to my best friend and editor Fátima telling her what I'm about to do. Somebody needs to know in case anything goes wrong even if it is hours later when the power returns. Then I pull on my raincoat, the wind would blow an umbrella inside out, and dash through the pummelling rain to the shed beside the house for a rope. It seems like the sensible thing to do.

Coiled rope in hand, I slip-slide my way down the lawn with ski slope-like slick grass and mud. The wind whips my hood back and I'm drenched, but I keep my eyes on the glowing headlamps. As I get closer, I see the car bonnet first in the stream. The lights are half submerged by fast flowing muddy water gushing around the car.

'Hello!' I shout but I'm drowned out by the keening horn and another flash of lightning and crack of thunder.

I inch my way forward, shining the meagre light from my phone into the cabin. The airbags have deployed and all I see is their white shape pressed against the fractured glass. I thought they were supposed to deflate after an accident.

Either way, somebody must be inside. I'm glad I brought the rope now because it would be impossible to safely get to the car any other way. I scramble back up the slope to the nearest tree, a willow, and tie the rope around it. It's difficult in the dark and the rain and the steam-train roar of the wind but my cold numbed fingers finally succeed in tying a knot. I pull on it to make sure it's firm, then tie the rope around my waist and head back to the car.

I'm praying the door isn't locked as I reach towards it, while the rushing stream pulls at my legs and the waves push up to my waist. At first the cold, wet metal doesn't budge as I pull with all my might. Then it gives with a click and falls open. The airbags deflate to reveal a man slumped against the steering wheel.

'Thank you,' I see him mouth as he turns his head towards me.

'Are you okay?' I shout.

The question feels stupid. His face is swollen. Blood has flowed from what looks like a broken nose making the lower half of his face particularly gruesome.

He reaches down to undo his seatbelt and nearly falls out of the car. I just manage to grab him but I'm worried. He is bigger and heavier than me. I'm not sure I can get him up the slope.

I pull his arms over my shoulders and shout, 'Hold on tight.'

He grabs his wrists to keep his grip around me and I pull hand over hand on my rope, out of the sucking water and up the bank. My feet slip out from under me and we both fall, face down as we reach the tree. He groans. I feel like I might suffocate.

Then he rolls off me and tries to get back onto his feet. I untie myself and do my best to help. The storm has calmed down a bit. The lightning has receded to distant flashes and the rain is easing. I wrap my arm around the man's waist, he puts his arm over my shoulder and we stagger and slip up to the house.

'Here, sit,' I say as we reach the kitchen door and wobble the short distance to a dining chair.

'Thank you,' the man says.

I can barely see him in the dark so I turn on my phone's torch. I'm a bit worried by how soaked the phone has got. I'm more worried by how pale the man looks.

'Do you not have light?' he asks.

'The power's gone down. But I have candles,' I say rummaging in the cupboard under the sink.

I emerge with a handful of candles that I press into my grandmother's old candelabra and then have to dig through a couple of drawers for matches. Eventually I have the candles lit and can see the man's face better.

'I'm Doroteia,' I say.

'Genaro,' he says. 'Could I use your phone? I need to make an urgent call.'

'I'm sorry, but the power is down and even the mobile network isn't working.'

He swears and pats all his pockets, maybe looking for his phone, but it seems he can't find it. I fetch some towels and bring a facecloth as well.

'You should probably clean that blood off your face,' I say handing him the facecloth and a bowl of water. 'I tried calling 999 when I saw the crash but I couldn't get through. I'm worried you may need medical help. I heard head injuries—'

'I'm a surgeon,' he says as he wipes at his face. 'And I was on call when a tree came down across the road. I swerved to miss it and...'

'I see.'

I wonder what I'm supposed to do. I've realised that both Genaro's knees are bleeding as well. That probably explains why he had difficulty walking.

'Can you get me to the hospital?'

'Oh,' I say because the solution is suddenly so simple. Why didn't I think of it? 'Of course. But don't you want to get dry first?'

'There isn't time.'

'Well... take a towel anyway,' I say.

'I'll need your hand,' Genaro says holding his out.

I take quite a lot of his weight, and he groans as he gets to his feet. He also says nothing as we make our way along the concrete path that leads to my driveway. Thankfully, the rain has eased, leaving only heavy drops from saturated trees.

I help Genaro into the car and as I'm starting up I say, 'Which hospital?'

'São Sebastião,' he says and starts towelling himself off while I head for the highway into Lisbon.

I turn the heating on full blast hoping it will dry us and because I'm shivering with cold and probably shock.

The moment the first lights appear from the surrounding houses Genaro says, 'Can I use your phone?'

It doesn't sound like a request and he's holding his hand out. I suppose doctors are used to giving orders. I fish in my pocket and hand it over giving him the PIN at the same time.

He grunts a thanks and calls the hospital.

'It's Professor Genaro,' he says. 'Has the patient been prepped for the operation?'

I can't hear the answer, my car is rather old and noisy.

'I won't be able to operate. I was in an accident, so assign Andrews. I'll talk him through everything he needs to know. I should be at the hospital in...' He turns to look at me.

'Half an hour,' I say.

Genaro nods and spends the rest of the journey on the phone talking to the other surgeon. At one point I realise Genaro is now guiding an operation. It sounds like an accident victim with head trauma.

That sort of thing makes me queasy. I can cope as long as I know it's fiction. But this isn't. Somebody's life is on the line.

A pair of orderlies are waiting for Genaro as I drive into the emergency entrance just behind a howling ambulance. An orderly helps Genaro into a wheelchair and runs off, pushing the chair at speed.

I'm about to drive off when I realise he was still talking on my phone when he left. Another ambulance has just arrived though so I give up and head home.

The next day a beefy tow truck appears to winch the doctor's car out of the stream. I try, unsuccessfully, to contact Genaro to ask for my phone. In the end I explain to an unhelpful receptionist all about who I am and how I know their surgeon. I leave my contact details but I'm thinking it's probably lost to me and I'll have to get another one. It's an unpleasant additional expense and, on top of it all, I'll have to get a new SIM card.

A couple of days later, I still haven't decided on a new model, when there is a tap at the kitchen door.

'Oh... Dr Genaro,' I say, surprised to find the man on my doorstep, using a crutch and with a large plaster over his nose. 'You look a lot better than last time.'

An eyebrow goes up and he holds out my phone.

'Sorry it took so long to get it back to you.'

'Thank you,' I say and he nods, apparently waiting for something. 'Would you like to come in for a coffee? You came a long way just to return a phone that could have been couriered.'

He tilts his head as he considers. It gives me time to give him a closer look. He's what I would call ruggedly good looking, with dark hair and a five o'clock shadow.

'Thanks, I'd like a coffee.'

He steps into the kitchen but looks ill at ease, glaring at the table that is littered with Christmas cards and where I've set up my computer.

'Sit,' I say and pull out the kitchen chair.

'I looked you up.' He has a cold tone, and even though he's seated it still feels like he's looking down at me. 'I discovered you're an author.'

He reminds me of all my disapproving teachers and my father rolled into one. But I refuse to be intimidated by somebody I rescued.

'I am,' I say and give him what I hope is a serene smile conveying that I am successful and happy.

'It isn't what I usually read, but it was well written.'

I'm pouring hot water over the coffee grinds but I come to a stop and put the kettle down.

'You read one of my books?'

I'm astonished. I write historical romance and I can't even imagine most men, let alone this rather cold individual, reading one of my books.

'It put me to sleep quite effectively,' he says in the same emotionless tone he's been using up till then.

'You do realise that isn't a compliment, don't you?'

I have to ask, because he doesn't seem to have noticed.

He actually looks surprised.

'I'm... sorry.'

It seems like he's not used to apologising either.

'So... how much of it have you read?'

'The whole thing. Once I start something, I finish it.'

'But you haven't had much time. You must read quickly,' I say as I place a mug of coffee in front of him, and push the sugar bowl from the middle of the table towards him.

He ignores the sugar and takes a sip of the coffee.

'I learned how to speed read at university.'

I take the sugar back and ladle a teaspoon into my mug. I resist the urge to justify my unhealthy food choices.

'Um... I probably shouldn't ask, but the patient you operated on that night are they...'

'They'll be fine,' Genaro says and sounds much more like a cool clinical doctor.

'So you're a neurosurgeon.'

'The best in the country.'

He says it like it's a fact and he doesn't even seem to have any pride in it.

'That's very impressive.'

I glance down at my laptop and my almost complete twelfth novel. I don't really have time for a conversation.

'I'm not very good with people,' Genaro says. 'I prefer them when they're unconscious on the operating table.'

'Ah.'

I'm uncertain what else to add or even why he said what he said.

'It seems to me, from your book, that you understand people very well.'

I laugh and shake my head.

'I hope I do. At least, I'm happy when my readers feel like I've portrayed something they feel is truthful.'

'You're also very attractive,' Genaro says in that same cool, emotionless voice.

I stare at him, processing. I'm in at-home-author-mode. My hair is a mess, I'm wearing shapeless comfortable writing clothes, no shoes, and two pairs of socks on each foot one of which has a hole over the big toe.

'Ha ha, is that so?' I say eventually because he doesn't seem to feel the need to break the silence.

'My colleagues have told me I should get a girlfriend. They think that will humanise me. Most of them are dating or married to nurses or other medical professionals but I don't want—'

'Wait,' I say holding out my hand to make doubly sure he stops. 'You've researched me and come over because you're looking for a girlfriend? Seriously?'

'You acted promptly to save me, so you're competent, and you have a high emotional quotient which I hope to learn from. You also appear to be single.'

'I don't go out much,' I say staring at this man.

I'm astonished but not repulsed. In fact, I'm intrigued. He is perfect novel fodder. I wish I could record this conversation.

'The only thing I fail at as a surgeon is my bedside manner. I usually have a colleague or nurse deal with the patients pre- and post-surgery otherwise... I get complaints.'

'From the patients?'

'Removing emotion from the operation ensures my judgement isn't impaired, and they have a better outcome. Patients don't seem to understand that.'

'I see.'

'I am very busy and don't like to waste time. It would be convenient if you'd agree to be my girlfriend as soon as possible.'

I nearly spray my mouthful of coffee across the table in surprise.

'I am also very busy. I have an end-of-year deadline on this book,' I say tapping my computer. 'And I'm not sure it would be convenient for me to be interrupted for dates.'

Genaro nods as if considering, leans back in the chair and his gaze sweeps across the kitchen taking in the frayed appearance.

'I am very wealthy.'

'I imagine you must be,' I say aware that he's thinking that makes him a catch.

He isn't wrong.

'Are you renting?'

'So what if I am?'

Now I am ticked off. This is too much of an intrusion.

'Why did you choose Sintra?'

'I like the quiet, and the forest.'

'Me, too.'

'Oh, you live in Sintra?'

I feel foolish saying it as I realise he must have been coming from his home when he had the accident.

He nods.

'You could save a considerable sum if you moved in with me. My house is warmer and more spacious.'

I'm back to being fascinated at how this conversation has accelerated to moving in. Nobody would believe me if I had my hero do this.

'You don't even know me. If I was to move in, which I absolutely will not be doing, you might discover you hate me.'

'But it would be more time efficient.'

'There is more to life than convenience and efficiency.'

Genaro tilts his head as if considering.

'You could teach me about that.'

'Why would I?'

'I'm sure a relationship could be mutually beneficial. For example, there are certain events that are difficult to avoid, like the staff Christmas party. At these times it would be convenient to have a date. You must have similar situations.'

He has hit on the singleton's dilemma. Even for somebody as apparently disinterested in social convention as Genaro, having a date for work dos, somebody to accompany you to friends' parties and even someone to go on holiday with are all little points of pressure that make me think having a boyfriend would be handy.

Genaro also looks pretty determined. There must really be something about me that he likes, because with his looks, status and money, there are surely plenty of women willing to go out with him. It makes me feel oddly flattered. Once the swelling from his broken nose goes down, he'll also look way more appealing.

'I really do need your help.'

He looks vulnerable as he says it and I realise he's being sincere in his own odd way.

'I tell you what, let's try one date — your work do or mine — and see what happens.'

Genaro looks surprised but also a shade pleased.

'You won't regret it.'

'You better make sure I don't,' I say as a thrill of nerves and excitement run through me.

I can't believe I'm doing this. I've avoided relationship for a long time as they always get too complicated. Maybe this hyper-reserved man is exactly what I need.

11th December

ERICA AND THE GENUINELY NICE MAN

I stroll down the drive absorbing the atmosphere and getting a sense of my surroundings. One reason I love my job is that I get to see inside some of the oldest and fanciest homes in Portugal. The one I'm currently approaching is a yellow and white wedding cake-like palacio on the Marginal overlooking the River Tagus where it opens out to the Atlantic Ocean. To the left, through a summery overgrown garden, are the pastel shaded homes of Lisbon banked up across a series of hills, with the Golden Gate-lookalike bridge sweeping across the river. To my right is the Portuguese riviera, a string of beaches lined with grand houses, hotels and even a casino.

A virginia creeper makes a green cave of the portico and it takes a moment for my eyes to adjust sufficiently to find the doorbell — an ancient white ceramic stud-like button. I push it hard and am relieved to hear the bell trilling inside.

I take a deep breath, preparing myself. Up till now, I'd only been in contact with my client via e-mail.

'Yes?' says a dumpy woman in a black dress with frizzy dyed black hair pulled into a bun, as she looks me up and down.

'Good morning,' I say, holding out my card. 'I have an appointment with Mr Leonel Manso at 10. I'm Erica Werneck, the arts restorer.'

The woman looks the card over sceptically.

'Mr Leonel didn't say anything about an appointment.'

'Didn't he?'

After years of dealing with the staff of wealthy people, whose main role is to block access to their employers, I have developed a few rules of my own. One of them is that I have no duty to explain. I had an appointment and that is that.

The woman gives me a look: thwarted of her morning's entertainment.

'Follow me.'

Old houses are frequently quite dark, especially when the windows are shrouded with vines, so it's difficult to see much of the hall and wide, stone-floored corridor, except that the place is well maintained. It seems this owner has more cash than many heirs of dwindling fortunes, which is reassuring.

'Mr Leonel, there's an Erica Werneck to see you,' the woman announces as she steps into a large study with a breath-taking view of the ocean.

A surprisingly young man slams his newspaper shut and leaps from the sofa to greet me, leaving inky smudges as he rubs his hands down his tan slacks.

'How do you do?' he says, holding a hand out in greeting.

Aside from oligarchs who've been buying up many of the grander houses in Lisbon, I rarely have young clients. This man looks about my age, average height, slim build, light brown hair and blue-grey eyes. Nothing exceptional except for the warm, welcoming smile.

'Mr Leonel, it's nice to finally meet you,' I say as I shake his hand.

He'd gone for a relaxed grip, not too tight, not too limp. It reflects a considerate person.

Then I look around the room. It's comfortable, with old squishy sofas arranged around the window for the best view, the newspaper-strewn coffee table between them. An ancient black carved wooden desk, shelves and shelves of books that look like they haven't been touched in years and, on the back wall, the mural I've come to inspect.

'Yes, that's it,' Leonel says, drifting deeper into the room. 'The damp problem has been resolved on the outside wall, but the plaster has bubbled and turned crumbly, and what with the banging from the other side when they redid the foundations, more of the mural has fallen away.'

'Yes I see,' I say and crouch down to inspect the base of the wall where things are always worst. The decay here is so great only the bricks remain. 'The best way to preserve the image is to photograph the whole thing, remove the old mural, re-plaster and paint a replica. Seeing this in the flesh, so to speak, I'm afraid I was right: the original mural is beyond saving.'

'It was a favourite of my mother's,' Leonel says with a sigh, which he quickly banishes with another charming smile. 'Never mind, I'm sure she'd prefer something new rather than a patched job.'

'As long as that's what you want.'

Clients have all sorts of reasons to preserve murals. Some for the historical integrity of their home, some for prestige and some for memories. Leonel had already informed me that his parents died in a car accident when he was young, and the mural was something he associated with his mother.

'I should have realised sooner what a terrible state it had fallen into,' Leonel says, and then gives an apparently unconcerned shrug. 'I have complete faith in you, Miss Erica. How long do you think it will take?'

I examine the condition of the wall, the state of the plaster and the size of the mural. It's reminiscent of the frescoes of Pompeii with a red background, a floral wreath surrounding an image of Pan playing his pipes for a troop of dancing nymphs. Fortunately, everything is clear enough for an accurate replica.

'Six months, possibly longer. It's a time-consuming project. But it will be done before Christmas.'

'This is my study. Will I be able to keep using it while you work?'

The question surprises me. Most clients hate being disturbed and usually avoid me like the plague. To be honest, I prefer that. It means I can also get on without interference.

'Aside from when I remove the plaster, which will be noisy and dusty, the rest is pretty quiet.'

'Excellent. Then I'll go away for a short break while you do that bit.'

Going away meant flying to Venice, I learned from the housekeeper, Maria Anna. Pretty much every woman over fifty in Lisbon is a Maria something. She warmed to me after she realised her boss was happy with me. Now she stops in at regular intervals to ply me with coffee and a dangerous selection of chocolate-coated biscuits from the local bakery.

She's also very fond of gossip and is delighted to have a brand new audience.

'It's a very quiet house,' I say one morning as I inhale the rich scent of coffee rising from my delicate gold and blue cup.

'Hah! It's quiet now because Mr Leonel is away, but you'll see the moment he gets back the house will swarm with people.'

'It will? I thought Mr Leonel lived on his own.'

'He wishes he lived on his own,' Maria Anna says, and leans forward as if to impart a secret. 'Actually, he likes people, and going out to see friends. But he doesn't want to be surrounded by family.'

'He doesn't?'

'Mr Leonel is far too kind hearted,' Maria Anna says, and leans back with a nod as if this explains everything.

'He does seem very considerate.'

'He's a pushover and the whole family takes advantage of him. The worst are the two tias.'

'His aunts?'

'His great aunt from his father's side, and his mother's oldest sister. When Leonel's parents died, there was a huge debate about what to do with him, and how he was going to be brought up.'

'I see. Were you there at the time?'

'I have been the housekeeper here since before Leonel was born.'

'So who landed up taking him in?'

'All of them, he started at his Aunt Letinha, for a while, then his Aunt Belisa demanded that he stay with her, then his uncle on his father's side weighed in and that's how it went, round and round until he went to university.'

I had a hard time reconciling what sounded like good news with Maria Anna's disapproving expression.

'At least they cared about him.'

'Cared!? Wanted a share of his money! Mr Leonardo, Mr Leonel's father, was really clever. He made millions and bought this palacio. The rest of the family leached off him and now do the same with Mr Leonel. Thank goodness he has a canny lawyer looking after his inheritance or he wouldn't have a cent left. As it is, the family is always getting stuff out of him.'

This last comment proved to be true. No sooner had Leonel returned from Venice when a never-ending stream of family members descended. The first two appear as I'm showing Leonel my next steps.

'I'll use a projector to throw an image onto the wall, and I'm sketching the pattern from that,' I say as a pair of teenage girls waltz into the room. I assume that they're twins. At least they have done their hair differently, so there's something to tell them apart.

'Cousin Leonel, you're back!' the girl with the ponytail says.

'Ah, Anabela and Analisa,' Leonel says with a smile that doesn't quite reach his eyes. 'What brings you here?'

'Mom said we can't get the new iPhone,' the girl with the braids says.

I can't figure out which is which.

'The new iPhone? Didn't you just buy new phones?'

'That was a year ago,' Ponytail says rolling her eyes as she flops onto the sofa, lying back and gazing at the ceiling.

'The new iPhone has a pink version, see?' Braids says, and holds her phone up so Leonel can see the screen. 'Buy it for us, Cousin Leonel. Go on, we'll never ask for anything else again. I promise.'

Even I can tell there isn't an ounce of sincerity in her words.

'Alright,' Leonel says and hands over his credit card with no appearance of dismay. Then he gives me a more sincere smile and says, 'Where were we?'

The twins disappear after buying phones and a ton of accessories. I assumed they were going home, but catch snatches of conversation from them in the distance for a while after that.

Two days later, a fearsome woman with steel grey hair done up in a loose bun sails into the room. None of them, as far as I can tell, ever give prior notice of their coming, or bother to knock.

'Aunt Letinha,' Leonel says, so surprised he knocks over his coffee cup and ignores the trickle of brown-black liquid that pools on his morning paper.

'Leonel, I'm sending your cousin Plácido to stay with you. He just got into the Economics University down the road, and it will be cheaper for him to stay here than in the hostel.'

'P.Plácido?' Leonel says faintly.

'You could use the company and he could use an older man to guide him.'

'But Aunt, Plácido always does exactly as he pleases.'

'Honestly, you're thirty-five years old, you're more than capable of controlling an eighteen-year-old. Live up to your name, for the love of God.'

'My name means a man from Leon,' Leonel says mildly. 'My father's name was related to lions.'

'Oh,' the aunt says, momentarily thrown.

Then she notices me and gives me such a fierce look that I hastily go back to my drawing.

Next is the second aunt. She has the same mid-brown hair as Leonel and the same grey eyes. She also seems milder, but her request is equally outrageous.

'Your uncle has started a new business,' she begins as she plops onto the sofa.

'Another one?' Leonel says.

'The market for cork shoes is growing and we have an excellent head start with our land in Alentejo. It's full of cork oaks.'

'I see.'

I guess Leonel has heard this kind of thing before because he goes entirely blank.

'We just need an investor and you would be perfect.'

'You'll have to check with my lawyer. I'll take his advice on whether it's worth investing. You know he won't let me if there is no chance of the company making money.'

'Honestly, you've got a degree in economics as well. You should be able to see what a brilliant investment this would be. Besides, you're old enough to make these decisions on your own now.'

'But you know I never do,' Leonel says with a placatory smile.

'I don't know why I bother,' Belisa says and springs to her feet. 'I'll send you all the information so you can send it to your lawyer.'

Then she flounces off, and a moment later I hear the front door slam.

'Wow,' I mutter under my breath.

'My uncle is always coming up with new companies,' Leonel says.

It makes me jump because I hadn't meant to be overheard.

'I'm sorry, it's none of my business. But for what it's worth, I think you did the right thing. It's your money. You can do what you please with it.'

Leonel actually looks surprised, as if nobody had ever said that to him before.

It's strange working with Leonel around. He has a set routine. He reads the newspapers in the morning, which I find odd. I thought everyone had gone online. He drinks a coffee with a single biscuit. Thank god he's returned, so Maria also rations me to a single biscuit. Then he heads to the gym and afterwards eats lunch with friends.

In the afternoon he's back, deeply absorbed in his phone, but just as frequently staring out of the window taking in the view. Sometimes he strolls over to peer at my painting and murmurs that it's looking good. Occasionally I sense him watching me, but he looks away if I turn around. It's peaceful, but I wonder why he does so little. The life of this rich man seems rather boring.

Cousin Plácido's arrival puts paid to the peace. He's anything but placid and wanders around half-dressed, his music blaring through his open bedroom door. He seems to always be eating and leaves a trail of crumbs wherever he passes. He also has a horde of loud friends who behave as if they are in their own home.

But even I'm astonished when he and three of his mates stroll into the study and plonk themselves on the sofa. Leonel had left earlier than usual to go to the gym. I suspect to avoid his cousin.

The music's blaring and the guys are shouting over the noise about the fantastic night they had, their female conquests and excessive drinking. Plácido had apparently passed out on the beach and would have been swept out to sea if his friends hadn't dragged him home. The noise and the chat make it impossible to work and I finally snap.

'You!' I say, pointing a quivering finger at Plácido. 'Have you no manners or are you too stupid and inconsiderate to realise that you are disturbing my work?'

Plácido blinks at me as if it's the first time he's noticed I was there.

'This is my house. I can do what I like here.'

The cheek of the kid. His family isn't even well off. I've learned from Maria that Plácido's family is firmly middle class.

'This is not your house. It belongs to your cousin, but you show neither him nor this house any respect. You're fortunate to live here for free, and instead of being considerate, you behave like a slob.'

I might have said more, but at that moment, I realise Leonel has returned and is watching the exchange in astonishment.

'Leonel,' Plácido says, 'can you believe this woman?'

Leonel frowns, and for a moment, I think blood will be thicker than water.

'She's not wrong. You're disrupting her work, so please leave.'

'But she's just some hired—'

'Plácido, behave yourself or I'll send you home.'

Plácido gasps and flounces out. His friends follow, grinning sheepishly.

'And turn off the music,' Leonel says to his retreating back.

'I'm sorry. I shouldn't have said anything.'

I'm certain I went too far. Leonel gives me a vague smile that thankfully reaches his eyes.

'It's my fault for letting the situation get out of hand. I'm sorry you were forced to speak up.'

'You looked very manly putting your foot down.'

I'd been surprised that Plácido complied, since Leonel didn't even raise his voice.

'Ah, that was just shock value. He'll go back to ignoring me in no time.'

'What will you do then?'

'Mmm,' Leonel says at his vaguest, 'send him home?'

Leonel gives a slightly embarrassed smile, then sinks into his usual spot on the sofa and takes out his phone.

I'm struck by the impression that Leonel might not be the pushover I'd thought him.

Plácido must feel the same. While the music volume slowly inches up over the next few weeks, no friends come over, and no crumbs are distributed, nor does he come back to the study.

Aunt Belisa returns, though, weighed down with a cardboard box filled with files.

'Everything to do with your uncle's new business,' she says, and mops her brow with the back of her hand.

'I'll look it over.' Leonel says in his usual neutral tone.

'Honestly, there's no need. You can see how much effort your uncle has made with all of this. Everything adds up.'

'I'm sure it does.'

It may be because I've spent so much time in Leonel's presence, but I just know he's in no mood for an extended debate.

'Excuse me, Leonel,' I say as I turn and give Belisa a smile. 'Remember we were going to look into that new blue paint today?'

He looks blank for a moment, then he smiles.

'Of course, such an important detail. I'm sorry Aunt Belisa but we have to go.'

She looks disgruntled but merely says over her shoulder, 'Don't forget to call me.'

'I won't.' Leonel follows her to close the study door, then says, 'Blue paint? I'm sorry. Did I forget something?'

'Actually, I should apologise and mind my own business. But you looked like you didn't feel up to being badgered and I could help so...'

'Very clever,' Leonel murmurs.

The following day, he goes to Paris.

I might not have put two and two together if one of the awful twins didn't say something. They're hanging around in the study when Leonel gets back from his trip.

He gives me a bright smile and says, 'Here!' as he hands over a prettily wrapped parcel.

'For me?'

'Just a little something I picked up in Paris. No big deal,' he says, but he looks more excited than most people are when receiving a present. 'Open it.'

With his expectant expression, I feel nervous as I tug at the gold bow, especially as the twins come hurrying over.

'A gift! You actually bought somebody a gift, Leonel,' Pigtails says.

I have a suspicion they deliberately switch their hairstyles from day to day, but since they're so hard to tell apart, I couldn't swear to it. Leonel doesn't seem to have any difficulty knowing who's who, though.

I peel the tape off the paper and slip a wooden box out. Inside the box is a very fancy set of brushes.

'Good heavens. This is wonderful.'

'Is it?' Leonel asks, and he looks pleased. 'I bought it on a whim. I was just passing by and saw them and I thought, as you're an artist, you know.'

'These are great brushes, really popular with people in the know.'

I would have said that I was thrilled with the gift, whatever it was. I hate to let gift givers down, but this really is a lovely present. Leonel looks pleased too. He nods and strolls out with a decided spring in his step.

'He bought something on a whim?' Ponytail says. 'Never!'

'Never?' I ask.

'Leonel has never bought any of us a gift. Not unless we've asked for it.'

'Maybe that's because you ask too often?'

That gets the twins to exit, staring daggers at me. But I don't care. It seems Leonel likes me and I... I'm not entirely indifferent to his quiet charm either.

A few weeks later, I'm doubting my interpretation. Leonel either has no interest in me, or little experience of putting his feelings across. Aside from coming over to watch me at work more often, his behaviour is unchanged. I fluctuate through waves of doubt, certainty, double doubt, hesitant certainty and an attempt at indifference.

Because of my uncertainty, I land up watching Leonel more and learn a few surprising facts. The first is that he isn't just living off his inheritance. He actually makes money. I made this discovery through the arrival of an impressive woman who radiates certainty before she even opens her mouth.

'Stella,' Leonel says as he leaps up to give her a kiss to each cheek.

It's the first sign of genuine pleasure I've seen from him. Is she a girlfriend? Have I been wrong about his feelings for me?

'I've come to give you your share,' Stella says with a broad grin as she holds out a manila envelope.

'In cash?'

Leonel looks as astonished as I feel.

'It's all above board, don't worry,' Stella says. 'The necessary paperwork for your accountant is also in the envelope. I just wanted to make this a bit more special. From now on, I will pay the income from your investment straight into your bank.'

'I appreciate the gesture,' Leonel says, then turns to me. 'I invested in Stella's restaurant.'

'And supported me through the Covid crisis when I was sure we'd go under.'

'I'm glad you didn't,' Leonel says.

'Me too.' Stella beams at Leonel, gives him a hug and says, 'I'd best be off. I've got a couple more envelopes to deliver to Armando and Bernardo.'

'We were at school together,' Leonel says by way of explanation once Stella has left.

He has the air of a boyfriend who doesn't want any misunderstanding. I want to tease him about it, but I'm not sure what to say.

'So you invested in your friend, but not your uncle?'

'My uncle doesn't have a business head. Every company he starts either fails to get off the ground, or goes bust in under a year.'

'And you?'

'I'm an angel investor. All the start-ups I support have made money.'

'Wow, does your family know that?'

Leonel looked thoughtful and then shrugs.

'I don't keep it a secret,' he says with his slight smile.

You cunning thing, I think, as I turn back to my painting. He knows full well his family thinks him a non-entity, but it seems to suit him. Not only that, but the twins and Plácido must realise there's a line they can't cross with him, even if they give no outward indication of it.

With Christmas just around the corner, I finally finish the last highlight on the last flower of the last bit of frame.

Leonel, who's become twitchy lately, and who often looks like he's on the verge of saying something but chickens out at the last minute, hurries over as I say, 'It's done!'

'It's wonderful!'

'I used one of your brushes on the last fine detail.'

'Did you?' he asks and leans in to take a closer look as if he'd spot the distinctive brush work.

'So...' I say, 'I guess this is it?'

'Wait!' Leonel dashes off. 'I bought a bottle of champagne for the occasion.'

He returns with two crystal flutes and an extremely expensive-looking bottle. So is this it? I wonder as I watch Leonel wrest the cork from the bottle. It explodes with a loud pop, bounces off the ceiling and wizzes past my work.

'Watch out! It's not dry yet. Talk about a lucky miss.'

'Have a drink,' Leonel says, grins sheepishly and holds out a glass where the bubbles are still fizzing on the surface. Then he raises a glass in salute and takes a deep sip.

I do the same and decide now is my last opportunity.

'You know, I got the impression you kind of like me.'

'You did?' Leonel says, his eyes widening in surprise.

'And I kind of like you,' I add, because I hate leaving things hanging.

'Well, you're not wrong,' Leonel says with a mixed sigh and laugh.

'So the paintbrushes...'

'Yeah, very meaningful. Just like the twins said.'

'But then... nothing.'

'I'm sorry about that. I'm not very good at... that sort of thing. But in my defence, I was also waiting till you finished, so we didn't have that awkward contractor, boss thing going on.'

'Well then,' I say as I lean in towards him, 'I think this requires a kiss.'

'I'd like that very much,' Leonel says as he folds his arms around me and his lips touch mine.

12th December

EDDY & THE WOMAN IN THE RED DRESS

I'm riding the waves at Carcavelos beach just for fun, because now I can, even on a weekday. The feeling of freedom this gives me, of finally chucking off everything that was holding my spirit down, is phenomenal. But even euphoria can't protect me from the cold. As it's also growing dark, I decide this run will be my last.

I'm just lining up the wave when a flash of red on the rocks catches my eye. There's a woman in a flowing red dress standing at the edge of the rocky outcrop that pokes out into the bay, brilliantly lit up by the setting sun.

'Hey!' I shout. 'Hey, get off the rocks, the tide's coming in!'

She doesn't react and I don't know whether it's because the crash of the waves drowns out my voice or if she's ignoring me. Either way, she's minutes from being washed away if I do nothing. I paddle across the current towards her, shouting, but she doesn't react. It's past the hours when the lifeguards are around and it's beyond their usual area of vigilance, anyway.

'Hey, hey!' I bellow, using every ounce of energy.

A couple of surfers notice and start following me. They've seen the woman too and add their voices to mine. I'm close now, still shouting at the top of my lungs. I daren't get too near or I'll also be washed onto the rocks and then there'll be two of us in trouble. But I have to work hard to keep in line with the woman, zigzagging back and forth as the waves roll relentlessly on.

An additional two surfers join us and we give a combined and mighty, 'HEY!'

The woman jumps and spins around.

'Get off the rocks,' I shout and wave frantically with both arms, my fellow surfers doing the same.

At this distance, all I can see is a white face with a look of blank confusion. She doesn't move, though. Has she come here to kill herself? I can think of few more painful ways than getting shredded on the rocks and drowned.

'The tide is coming in! Get off the rocks.'

She finally registers why we're all shouting, turns and starts making her way back as the first of the waves breaks over the rocks and swirls about her feet. She stumbles, groping at a few barnacle-encrusted stacks and staggers forward, but the waves are getting higher and at the rate she's going, with that stupid long dress twisting round her legs and snagging, she's never going to make it.

'Keep an eye on her,' I say to the other surfers and ride a wave right onto the beach. I run for the rocks and start making my way out to the woman.

She's struggling, drenched now, with her fancy hairdo soaked and strands of blonde hair plastered to her forehead. Her makeup has streaked black lines down her face, but I can't tell if that's from tears or spray.

'It's okay, I'll get you out of here,' I say and reach out towards her.

'Help!'

She lunges forward and just manages to take my hand as a powerful wave smacks into the two of us. I yell and grip the rocky ground with my toes and hang on for dear life. We need to get out of here before the next wave breaks, so I pull the woman, more like a girl really, close, wrap an arm about her waist and hoist her nearly off her feet. She's either very light or the adrenaline's doing its job as I race across the rocks and back to the beach with the waves pounding into us.

'Ahhh,' I sigh with relief, as I put the woman down and bend over to catch my breath.

'Well done, man,' one of the surfers who'd come over to help says and gives me a high five.

Then he tilts his head towards my board that he'd pulled further up onto the beach.

'Thanks,' I say and turn to examine the woman.

My first inclination is to ask what the hell she was doing. But she looks shocked and is shivering and soaked through. What was once a fluffy red coat is now as bedraggled as her hair.

'Let's get you out of the wind. I've got a towel and some dry clothes I can lend you. My car isn't far away.'

She follows along without a word as I hoist my surfboard, wave a grateful farewell to my fellow surfers and head for the carpark. I open the back of my 4x4 and rummage around in the first of the plastic tubs with all my gear.

'Here, a towel,' I say, and hand it back without looking.

I hear a muttered, 'Thanks.'

It's always better when people start speaking. At least you know they're engaging with the world again.

I have a large poncho-like towel that I slip over my head so I can change out of my wetsuit without being done for indecent exposure. Then I rinse and towel off and scramble into my dry clothes. The woman, in the meantime, is just standing, wrapped tightly in the towel and looking like the proverbial drowned rat but at least alive enough to be shivering.

'My clothes will be too big for you but at least they're dry,' I say as I hand her the poncho so she can strip and I dig out my most figure-hugging long sleeved t-shirt and a pair of drawstring joggers from the other tub.

I wonder if I'll have to explain what the poncho is for because for a while she doesn't move. Then finally she pulls the soaked jacket off and lets it drop to the ground with a sodden plop. Next comes the dress, also discarded on the road.

'Shit,' I say as I spot her badly scratched ankles. 'Those uneven rocks are tricky, especially with the barnacles.'

Her red shoes, that look like they must have cost a fortune, are also wrecked. I hand her my rinsing bottle and fresh towel and open a side compartment in the boot where I keep my first aid kit. I'm nothing if not prepared. Silent as the woman is, she works quickly and is dressed by the time I've tidied everything away.

'Okay,' I say and tap the back of the boot. 'Sit up here and I'll see to your wounds. Do you have any additional injuries?'

She shakes her head so I wash the scratches around her ankles with what remains from my big rinsing bottle, then apply disinfectant and bandage everything. At least the gash isn't so deep that it needs stitches. She's got nice shapely ankles, I think, feeling a bit like a Victorian perv.

'All done.' I scoop her clothes up, shove them into a plastic bag and drop them into my boot. 'Now let's get you into the car and warmed up.'

She gives me a dubious look, which is at least better than the hopeless one she had before. Elena, my older sister, once went on a rant with a very complete list of what women do to keep themselves safe. Getting into a stranger's car is high on the list of what not to do.

'I'm Eddy,' I say, holding my hand out. 'Eddy Zeller.'
'Zeller?'

She sounds surprised. I guess she's heard of the family name, which is interesting. Our family is discreet. Outside of the circle of well to do, we are relatively unknown.

'I'm Alice Giralt.'

She says it like I'll know who she's talking about, and I do. Same circle of the super-rich. So now she's at least okay to get in the car. I start the engine and flip the heating up to maximum. Then I take out my flask of coffee. I pour half a lid full for Alice and take a sip out of the flask myself so she knows it's safe to drink. She sits, hands wrapped around the lid, staring into the black coffee.

'Are you okay?'

She looks up and gives me a fleeting smile.

'I must look pretty stupid, huh?'

I shrug.

'We all have our stupid days.'

'Yeah, well, I've had a pretty stupid um...' she looks up into the distance, her lips moving. 'Six months. Yeah, it's been six months.'

I like to think I know women quite well. Aside from my fiery sister and my all too sensible sister-in-law, I've had a fair few girlfriends, so I reckon I know what's going on.

'Bad boyfriend?'

'Bad fiancé.'

'Ah, that is much more serious. What did he do?'

'Fooled me completely, and I nearly fell for it. My uncle warned me about him and I ignored him at first.'

'He told you to stay away, huh?'

I don't know a lot about the Giralt family, except that Mr and Mrs Giralt died leaving their daughter in the charge of Xavier Tavares, another of my brother Armando's powerful friends.

'He threatened to withhold my inheritance.'

'That's tough. I've had a similar threat dangled over me.'

'I was all ready to tell him to go to hell and bring my wedding forward. But then Uncle Xavier sent me an email apologising, and telling me to do what I want, but just to look over the information he'd gathered.'

'That's a surprising change of heart.'

'Yeah, I think his new girlfriend has something to do with that,' Alice says while staring out of the car at the dark ocean beyond that's only visible in the spotlights on the beach. 'Anyway, even

though I didn't mean to, because I trust... I trusted my fiancé .
In the end, I couldn't contain my curiosity.'

'That's understandable, and not that I want to take sides, but
when you have a lot of money, you have to be careful. I've had
any number of dubious women try to take me for a fool, too.'

Alice nods and finally looks up and sees me properly. She's
looking prettier now that her face has regained some of its
colour.

'The jerk has two girlfriends on the side. Can you believe
that? Two! And he's a gambler who keeps losing money.'

'That is bad.'

'And you know what else he did?' Alice says, her eyes
flashing. Anger has taken over from grief. 'When I said we need
to meet to discuss the wedding, he suggested the Estoril Casino.
I mean, I hadn't told him yet that I knew about his gambling
habit, but isn't it a bit much to meet your fiancée at a casino?
And to already be playing when I arrive and to tell the cashier
that I'll pick up his tab.'

'Sounds like he felt very sure of your affection.'

'Yeah,' Alice says and sinks in on herself again. 'He had good
reason for that. It's not the first time we'd been to the casino,
but I thought it was fun, you know. Uncle Xavier never does
things like that.'

'There's a fine line between fun and addiction.'

'That's for sure. But this time, I stood up for myself and I
demanded he tell me about his other women and how much
money he keeps losing. And he blew up, screaming at me to not
be a controlling bitch, and just shut up and do what he tells me.'

'Jeez!'

That really is extreme and I've seen some pretty wild
behaviour in my time from gold diggers.

'Yeah, so I... just ran away. I jumped into a taxi and was going
to go see my uncle. But as we passed the beach, I just thought...
I need to clear my head. So I got out, and I went to the water's
edge. I was just really stunned, you know?'

It's hard to tell the colour of Alice's eyes in the light of the car, but they are big, innocent and suddenly very charming.

'I get that. Sometimes you just need some time to think. But next time, be a bit more aware of your surroundings.'

'I will.' Alice laughs and gives me a much warmer look. 'What about you? How come you were out surfing on a workday?'

'I recently quit my job.'

Even though I've told hundreds of people already, I still get a sense of relief saying it.

'Oh. I thought all Zellers work for the family firm.'

'Not anymore. It's what I was trained to do. I got my degree in a subject that didn't interest me at all for that same reason.'

'What a bummer.'

I laugh because Alice has just voiced how I always felt.

'Are you being encouraged into doing something you don't like?'

'Not at all,' Alice says and finally takes a sip of what must be lukewarm coffee by now. 'If anything, my uncle gives me too much leeway. For the last six months, I was wrapped up in romance and wedding planning. Maybe that was my project to keep me busy. Now I don't know. What do you do now that you've quit?'

'My first love, surfing. I'm about to go pro.'

'Did your family cut you off because of it?'

'My father threatened to, but thankfully my brother came to my rescue, as always. In more ways than one, because he told me to build up a pot of money of my own before I handed in my notice. And he also set up a sponsorship deal. I have to get the other half of the money, but it was a big help.'

'He sounds nice. Nothing like what I've heard about him.'

'He's misunderstood.' It always annoys me when people say bad things about my brother. I don't want Alice to be one of those people. That catches me up short. I'm pretty self-aware, and I've just realised I fancy this girl. 'How old are you?'

I'd been thinking teenager, but I don't think teenagers get married anymore. Do they?

'I'm twenty-one. How about you?'

'Twenty-six,' I say, grinning at her.

Girls only ask this kind of question if they're interested. In that case, the feeling is mutual.

'Listen, I know you're not dressed for it, but can I buy you a drink and maybe something to eat?'

'Here?' Alice says and looks out across the car park at the beach restaurants and bars whose lights are twinkling away.

'Yeah, why not?' I say. 'Then I promise I'll take you home.'

'Okay, I'd like that.'

My evening is shaping up nicely. Alice might still be upset about the dirtbag fiancé, but I like her. There's an indefinable something that feels different to all my past flings. With a little space and patience, we could have a glorious future together.

13th December

CAROLINA AND THE MAGICIAN

Treze, it's the name of the company. Thirteen in Portuguese. I'm standing at the entrance to a fancy office building, making sure the workmen get our meters high sign in place without leaving a scratch or smudge on the highly polished chrome.

'Takes you back, doesn't it?' Melchior says coming up beside me.

He has a knack for reading me, actually for reading anybody. It's his talent. I was remembering years ago when I was a high school kid and he'd just started his company.

'Why did you choose an unlucky number for your company name?' I'd asked him.

'Because it makes people stop and think, little one,' he'd said, 'and ask the question you're asking. And tell me about their misfortunes. That's when I show them how to overcome whatever is holding them back.'

'For money.'

'Of course. Man's got to eat, have clothes and shelter. Everything after that is a bonus.'

Well, this is the bonus now, owning an entire building with a sea view. The company itself only takes up the top two floors, the floor below is Melchior's new home, the rest is rental income.

'We've come a long way,' Melchior says, head thrown back, hands in the pockets of his figure-hugging brown trousers with the faint yellow grid.

It's his favourite suit. Black is too intimidating and grey too boring; blue pinstripe is conventional businessman; none of them gives off the right signal. Brown makes him approachable, and the grid adds a touch of daring, signalling to the client that this is a creative, slightly out of the ordinary person. Just the type you need to solve your big corporate problems.

Life hasn't always been this great. Melchior used to be our next-door neighbour in a tiny block of flats built so close to each other that my mother could hand things through the window to my aunt in the building opposite. Tourists would wander down our narrow lane taking photos saying, 'How charming!'

I couldn't understand English at the time, but I knew body language well enough to see that they liked our ancient suburb which spilled down the mountain below Lisbon's castle. I couldn't understand why. There were six of us in a two-bedroom apartment. We didn't have a single unchipped plate. Lightbulbs blew and took months to be replaced. All the taps had a permanent drip. The floorboards were loose and the plaster was cracked.

Because our place was so full, we kids often hung out in the corridor, the stairwell, or the narrow foyer of the building with all the other kids. And that's how I found out Melchior was a magician. He'd head out in the evening dressed in a dapper black suit, a red-lined cape slung over his arm, a black square suitcase in the other hand.

Naturally we all thought he had the most wonderful job in the world and demanded he do tricks for us before we'd let him leave the building. So he'd oblige and pull a coin out of a kid's ear or turn a wand into a row of knotted silk handkerchiefs, but it was only ever one trick. Somehow he always managed to slip away after just one. The other kids didn't notice, but I did.

'How do you do it?' I asked him one Sunday.

He didn't work on Sundays and I caught him in the afternoon coming back with his groceries.

'Do what?' he'd said without pausing as he unlocked his door and stepped inside.

He was about to shut me out so I launched myself at the gap and squeezed in just as the door snapped shut. There we were: me staring defiantly at him, Melchior looking surprised.

'How do you slip past all the kids with only one trick? No other adult gets out of the building that fast without beating us up.'

'So you noticed, did you?'

'Yep.'

'Good for you.'

I nodded, peering past Melchior. His apartment was emptier than I'd expected but spotlessly clean and with two boxes full of props.

'Can I look?'

Melchior shrugged, put his bag of shopping down, sat on the edge of his two-seater sofa, and took out a large silver coin. He said nothing as I worked my way methodically through one box and then the next. He just wound the coin about his fingers and made it vanish and reappear, first from one hand and then from the other.

'You're one of the kids from next door, aren't you?' Melchior said when I finished with the boxes.

I nodded and glanced at the wall that separated our house from his. We could hear my father shouting at my mother and slapping her about. The kids were quiet: either outside, like me, or in hiding. You did not want to get in my father's way when he was drunk and angry.

'Do you want some lunch?' Melchior said heading to the small kitchen.

'What are you having?'

'Vegetable soup and bread.'

'What kind of soup?'

'Caldo verde.'

'Does it have chouriço in it?'

'It does,' Melchior said with a solemn nod.

I liked that he didn't get impatient. My father would already have slapped me for asking too many questions.

'Okay then,' I said.

Looking back, I'm still embarrassed that I made it seem like I was doing him a favour when, really, a proper meal that I didn't have to fight over with my siblings and a place to hang out away from my mother and father was heaven.

And that's how our relationship began. First it was me just barging in at every opportunity. Then, to prolong my stay, I made Melchior teach me magic. At some point, I started sleeping over, curled up on his small couch. It happened so often that one morning I woke to find he had covered me with a blanket. This made me bolder, and I went around the building claiming Melchior as my own.

He neither encouraged nor discouraged, just left me to do as I wished. And when I finished high school, I demanded that he let me join his show and make me his assistant.

'You're too skinny,' Melchior said looking me over critically.

'Well... I can wear a dress rather than a leotard. A nice puffy dress with lots of sparkles like a fairy.'

Melchior laughed. He didn't do it often. By this time I had discovered, because I asked after noticing that he never had family come to visit, that he was an orphan. He'd run away from the orphanage quite young. More than this he wouldn't divulge. I suspected even his name wasn't his original one.

'Actually,' he said, 'I'm giving up the stage and opening a business.'

'A business,' I said as all my post school plans fell to dust. 'What kind of business?'

'One that helps people solve problems.'

'What kind of problems?'

'Anything.'

'What makes you think you can do that?'

'You know part of my act is mind reading, right?'

That was true, I'd seen the act many times. Melchior could just look at a person and know what they were thinking and why. He'd explained that it was actually body reading: facial expressions, hand gestures, posture and even clothing, but it was still uncanny how detailed he could get.

'So how does that help?'

'I can get to the actual root of the problem. Not just what people are telling me, but what they are really thinking. Companies in Great Britain are pioneering this stuff, working with actors and what not to improve business.'

'But then what am I going to do?'

Melchior held out his hand.

'What? What do you want?' I asked.

'Payment. If you want me to solve your problem, I require payment. You can be my first customer.'

This was typical Melchior. So, grumbling, I took out the collection of coins I had in my pocket and put the lot into his palm.

He gave me a triumphant smile and said, 'Thank you for being my first customer, Miss Carolina. The solution to your problem is quite simple, you can become my first employee. The pay will be terrible at the beginning, but I promise it will improve.'

'It did improve, didn't it?' Melchior murmurs as we walk through the grand foyer of our new building, past the massive, two storey-high Christmas tree to the glass lift that gives us a breath-taking view of the city and the sea.

'Beyond my wildest dreams. We now have some of the top companies in the country as our clients and I've gone from general dog's body to director of marketing.'

'Mmm,' Melchior says while giving me his weighing up look.

We've arrived at the top floor, beautifully decorated in light coloured wood furniture, modern impressionistic photographs and lots of plants. Everything is ready for the staff to join us on Monday. We turn left towards Melchior's new, glass-enclosed office that looks out across the harbour and the ocean beyond. I'm keeping slightly ahead of him so that he can't read my face. I can do little about the rest although I've learned a few tricks over the years.

'No,' Melchior says as we arrive at his office.

'You don't even know what I'm going to say,' I snap, suddenly angry.

I've been working myself up to this for months, maybe even years, and he shoots me down before I can say anything?

'You're going to tell me you love me.'

'I do.'

'I'm old enough to be your father.'

'I don't care, at least you know that too.'

'And I know what people have said and thought about us, especially when I let you stay at my apartment. A grown man and a girl... I was a fool to do it.'

'But you did.'

Melchior shrugged.

'I knew what went on in your home so I put up with the rumours.'

'I was really grateful to you for that and everything else you did for me. Compared to where my brothers and sisters and even my cousins landed up, my life has been miraculous.'

'You shouldn't mistake gratitude for love.'

'Come on.' I take Melchior's hand, even though he tries to avoid it. 'The omniscient CEO of Treze can't tell the difference between love and gratitude? Give me a break.'

'Are you sure you can?'

'I know I love you.' I step closer so that now I can smell his spicy cologne. 'And I know you've never had a girlfriend since we've been together.'

'Well... not entirely true,' Melchior says as he steps back and switches to staring over my shoulder. It's a technique he taught me to make a person harder to read.

'Near enough.' I step even closer so that now I can feel the warmth of his body and his breath on my cheek. 'You promised me a memorable Christmas. You said I could ask for anything for my gift.'

'You're asking for something I can't give you,' Melchior says but his fingers curl about my hand.

'I'm twenty-five now. I'm a competent professional and your business partner. I've grown up and I want you to acknowledge that and see me properly. I'm not your little one anymore.'

'I can certainly see that,' Melchior says although now he's staring at the ceiling.

'It look like you're trying very hard not to see.' I resist the urge to stamp on his toes even if it will force him to look down. Instead, I cup my free hand around his face and say, 'Please, Melchior, give me a chance.'

'You know, if this doesn't work out it will ruin our work relationship too, don't you?' he says but at least he's looking at me.

'Is that what's holding you back?'

'Maybe, plus the age gap, and... we both know I'm not great with personal relationships.'

This is true. Melchior has a wall between himself and the rest of the world. Maybe from his isolated youth, maybe because he can read people too easily.

'Do you really think, at this point, no matter what happens, you'll be able to push me away?' I say leaning so close that now we're touching and I can feel the rough tweed of his suit.

He tilts his head, considering, and a smile tweaks the corner of his mouth.

'Little Miss Carolina, always forcing her way in.'

That's all I need. I kiss him. Melchior wraps his free hand around my waist and pulls me closer and we kiss again. Relief floods in. We've broken the barrier. A new chapter starts here.

14th December

MANUEL AND LILIANA FACE OFF

I'm staring up at the stone and tiled facade of an eight story Novo Estado block of flats that I've come to view. This art déco building with a touch of fascist dictator in the design is a rare beast. First, because there aren't many buildings in this style. Second, because the heirs of the former owner have stipulated that they want to sell it to a Portuguese.

Since Lisbon has become a popular tourist destination, more popular than Venice, apparently, multinationals are snapping up any building of a decent size that comes on the market. Almost all of them get turned into hotels. I intend to keep it as private, rented accommodation.

Private rentals are also becoming scarce since so many apartments are being turned into Airbnb lets. It pushes up the rent on the remaining properties. As a resident of Lisbon, this appals me. As a landlord, I'm making a fat profit.

This won't necessarily be my biggest purchase. I've picked up a couple of modern blocks of flats. But it will be my most prestigious in a trendy part of Lisbon near the Gulbenkian museum and garden. If I manage to buy the building, I might even move into one of the apartments myself.

I chuckle at that idea. My parents couldn't even have dreamed of living in a place like this. Not that they know about my success. They kicked me out of the house when I turned sixteen. I'd already been working as a labourer for a builder friend of my father's for the previous two years. But at sixteen, I refused to hand my meagre pay over to my father because I didn't see why he got to drink my wages and only give me pocket money.

After that, I lived rough for a while and worked my way up from labourer to builder, saving every cent I earned. Finally, I had enough to buy a wreck of an old house. Lisbon is full of them. I did it up, sold it for a profit and bought another. On and on, until one day I woke up to find I'm a property mogul.

I check my phone for the time. I'm due to meet the lawyer representing the seller's family at 15:00. It's 14:55.

And then, a taxi pulls up at the curb beside me and Liliana Lee steps out. My first thought is: Impossible! My second, more swearword-filled one, is that it is all too possible. While the Lee family came to Portugal from Macau, they are surely Portuguese citizens and Liliana was probably born here.

She's slim, dressed in the height of fashion, with a fur-trimmed coat and astonishingly high stiletto heels. Her dead straight, pitch black hair is ruffled by the light winter wind as she gazes at me with the haughty expression a princess might give an inconvenient beggar.

I've had a long day of legal negotiations about a shopping centre my father wants to build. He'd promised me if I stood in for him for that I could have the afternoon off. Only to discover that he'd arranged a blind date for me, for the afternoon. I mean really, we might be of Chinese descent, but even in the motherland, arranged marriages are becoming less and less common. I can already guess what the man will be like: Chinese, and some sort of businessman. Looks, age or any of my personal preferences are ignored.

So I tell dad I'll go inspect a potential property I've had my eye on. If it's business, my father never stands in my way, thank goodness. But I'm not in a great mood. I've got a niggling headache and an inspection of my handbag informed me that my little pillbox was devoid of painkillers. So the last thing I need is to see him, Manuel Domingos.

It shouldn't be a surprise. He's a competitor, always snapping at our heels, but nowhere near our level. At least he's dressed relatively smartly today. I think he enjoys going about looking like a labourer in ragged workmen's clothes. It makes people underestimate him.

Today, while he's wearing jeans, they're new and paired with a new black coat. If I could stomach his company for even a minute, I might say he scrubs up well. He's also got the hard, lean physique of a labourer rather than the more rounded muscular look of a gym rat.

But he's proud that he's a self-made man and doesn't hide that his schooling was so limited he's practically illiterate. He usually goes around with a PA to do all his reading and writing, but that person is absent today.

He looks down on me because I had the full package: private education, American university, and a family business to inherit. Everything handed to me on a silver platter, he once said. The fact that I work damn hard is irrelevant because, as far as he's concerned, I never earned it.

'Good afternoon,' Manuel says, and he sounds as irritated as I feel.

'Hello, Domingos,' I say and turn away, cursing the lawyer for being late.

I consider coming back another day, then decide against it. I can't have Domingos thinking he intimidates me.

Then I spot the lawyer hurrying up the hill towards us. I looked him up. Their law firm is just a couple of blocks down.

'Sorry I'm late, I couldn't find the keys,' he says, puffing and leaning forward with a hand outstretched. 'I'm Fernando Raposo.'

After brief introductions, we follow him up the stairs and wait while he checks one key and then the next to find the one that will let us into the foyer. He talks as he works, his back to us, and not turning around to check whether we're listening.

'As you'll have seen, half the apartments are now empty, as we have not signed new tenants up after the owner's death. The rest of the tenants are on fixed term tenancies.'

I know all of this. It was in the sales info, but I don't bother stopping Fernando. At least while he's speaking, I can pay him all my attention and ignore Domingos. He's doing a pretty good job of ignoring me by running an expert eye over the foyer, probably estimating to the cent how much each tile and deco lampshade is worth.

I wonder what he's planning to do with the place. He usually keeps apartments as apartments, brings them up to a rentable standard and moves onto the next project. He is so lacking in imagination.

The building is in great shape despite its seventy-odd years of age. It's well maintained and, even at the current asking price, well worth going for. I risk a glance at Liliana. She's doing her best "attentive listening" to the lawyer who's lapping it up. There's nothing a man likes more than to have the undivided attention of a beauty. If I'm not careful, she's going to charm this building right out from under me.

So while the lawyer shows us the old-fashioned wrought iron lift, that needs work, the stairwell, one of the empty flats, then up to the roof to see the view and the communal space I try to make a personal connection with the man. I need him to remember me and think well of me. Business, after all, isn't company to company, but person to person.

It's an uphill struggle. Liliana is clearly way more appealing. I'm thinking I'll need to extend my evening and take the lawyer out to dinner when his phone goes off. He offers profuse apologies and shuffles off to one corner of the rooftop for a brief but intense conversation. Liliana and I accidentally lock eyes, then both of us look away, slowly, like fighting cats who've decided retreat is best.

'I'm really sorry, but I have to go,' the lawyer says when he hurries back. 'I can leave the keys if you want to carry on looking at the building, if you wouldn't mind dropping them off at our office afterwards.'

'Not a problem,' I say, holding out my hand.

It's actually great to be able to look a building over without the watchful eye of the seller.

'I'd be happy to drop them off,' Liliana says and intercepts the ring of keys.

The lawyer actually blushes as his fingers brush hers. Yep, this sale is slipping away.

'I want to check the basement,' I say as Fernando Raposo leaves.

My voice betrays more irritation than I'd intended, but this isn't so that I can be as far from Liliana as possible. The basement houses most of the utilities and these can be a hidden deal destroyer.

'I'll check it out too,' Liliana says, maintaining her cool, unflustered princess persona.

She can't fool me. Her dislike shows despite trying to be inscrutable. We get wordlessly into the lift, then stare in opposite directions as we descend to the ground floor. She's wearing perfume, something floral.

We step out of the lift and round the corner to the basement door. The click clacking of her heels on the marble floor sounds incredibly loud. It takes a moment of checking keys before she gets the right one. In the meantime, I look for something with which to wedge the door open.

'Leave it, it's fine,' Liliana says as I'm about to drag over an abandoned glazed pot plant container.

'I don't want to get locked in. It's one of those latch doors.'

'I have the keys. How can you get locked in?' Liliana asks, clearly exasperated.

The door opens with a rusty shriek and we make our way down the rough steps. In here it's bare concrete. The fluorescent lighting is flickering in an irritating way and the basement smells musty. This is not uncommon in Lisbon because of the high humidity.

The door slowly swings shut and closes with a click as we reach the bottom. A wave of panic washes over me, but I clench my fists to suppress it. There is no way I'll show any weakness in front of this woman.

She's all business and I will be too. I head for the utilities box and take out my phone. First to check it all out by the light of the torch, then to photograph the wiring and piping.

Liliana peers around me, probably seeing what I'm seeing.

'It's not too bad.'

'What will you do with the building if you buy it?' I ask, despite my better judgement.

'That's confidential,' Liliana says without looking at me.

She's taking pictures too. Not just the utility but the state of the concrete floor and walls. There's a pale discolouration that might indicate a leak somewhere. I'm annoyed that she spotted it before I did.

'Well, that seems to be it,' Liliana says. 'Are you finished?'

I want to get out of this locked room as quickly as possible. So, despite feeling I should be more thorough, I say, 'I'm done.'

We head back up the stairs, Domingos at the rear but keeping his distance, thank god. I take out the key and try to fit it into the lock.

'What's wrong?' Domingos asks after I've struggled for a few seconds.

'It won't go in.'

'Are you sure it's the right key?'

The flickering light has exacerbated my headache and I snap, 'Of course it's the right key.'

Even so, I check all the other keys before coming back to the one I knew was right all along.

'It feels like something is in the way.'

'Stand aside,' Domingos mutters.

He takes the key out of my hand and pushes it into the lock with considerably more force than I could or would dare to use. The key only goes halfway. So he proceeds to check all the other keys.

'I've already tried that,' I say, my annoyance growing.

He knows, he was peering over my shoulder the whole the time. His hand is shaking though, and I wonder why. I've never noticed them shaking before.

'I should have used that accursed plant pot.'

Domingos isn't looking at me, but it feels like he's blaming me. Then he takes his phone out again and shines the light into the keyhole.

'There's definitely something in there.'

He does the typical man thing of fiddling with the lock like he can fix it. I've had enough messing about. All I want is to go home, put my feet up and drink a glass of wine. I take out my phone and dial the lawyer and get an unpleasant beeping.

'I've got no signal, do you?'

I have to raise my voice because Domingos is pounding the lock with the side of his fist as if that's going to shake something loose.

'What?'

'Do you have a phone signal? Let's just call somebody to get us out.'

'Oh yes,' he says and looks at his phone. 'No, no signal.'

Domingos kicks the door a couple of times. It's metal-plated and he winces.

'Maybe there's a better signal somewhere in the basement,' I say as I start down the steps waving my phone in the air, my eyes fixed on the signal bars.

I assume I've arrived at the ground level and instead step into air. I land heavily and my shoe heel snaps, my foot twists and I go flying, arms wind-milling for something to grab onto. Then I smack into the concrete floor.

'Liliana!' Domingos shouts, bounds down the stairs and kneels beside me. 'Are you alright?'

I want to scream that of course I'm not alright, but my ankle, left elbow, right wrist and chin are all vying for the most-in-pain prize. I'm also humiliated.

'No,' I barely manage to squeak.

'Is anything broken?'

Domingos sounds genuinely alarmed.

'I don't know.'

I just want to curl into a ball, not answer questions, not try to get up, just get my breath back and pull myself together.

'Your ankle looks pretty bad. Do you mind if I touch it?'

'Uh huh,' I say while shaking my head.

He looks uncertain whether or not I've given him permission but decides I did, and I feel a sharp pain against my ankle.

'Ow. That hurts... a lot.'

'I don't think it's broken, though. Let me get you upright and I'll check the rest.'

The initial shock has worn off, so I'm okay with Domingos supporting my arm as I roll over and sit with my back against the bottom step.

'Your chin is bleeding,' Domingos says and starts feeling about his pockets.

'I have tissues in my bag.'

I wish more than ever that I had my painkillers, too.

Domingos fetches my bag which had flown across the basement and hands it to me. Then, while I'm digging around for my tissues, he pulls out a clean grey hanky and wraps it tightly around my ankle.

'I thought you said it wasn't broken.'

'It isn't. But you should bandage it to keep swelling to a minimum.'

'What were you, a Boy Scout?' I say as I finally find the tissues and pull one free.

'I take a first aid course every year. Just in case.'

'Yeah, I guess you didn't have the Boy Scout type of youth.' He stiffens, and I say, 'I didn't mean that as a criticism. I didn't do anything like that either. It wasn't my thing.'

'Ah,' Domingos says and shines his torch on my grazed wrist while I dab at my chin.

The tissue comes away with a lot of blood.

'Shit. Do you think that's going to leave a scar?'

Domingos stares at my face, tilting his head this way and that. I can't tell whether he's thinking I'm vain or checking the wound.

'It doesn't look too bad,' he says.

Then again, he's a builder. His hands are covered in the scars of cuts and nicks gained over the years. I'm not sure what counts as bad for him.

The lift comes to life beside us with a whine and a clank.

Domingos leaps up the stairs two at a time and bangs on the door and shouts, 'Hey, hey, can you hear me? We're trapped in here!'

He keeps going till the lift stops. It sounds like it's gone to the top floor. Domingos sighs and comes back down the stairs. He sits on the floor opposite me and looks me over once again.

'How do you feel?'

'Fine.'

I'm not used to Manuel Domingos being concerned. Usually, he looks annoyed and barely says two words. Now, in the flickering white neon that leaches everything of life, he looks extra pale, and maybe… I've been trying to put my finger on the emotion. It's not one I've seen from him before, but now I've got it.

'Are you scared?'

'What would I be afraid of?'

'I don't know. Not the dark, we've got light, even if it is irritating. Not small spaces because the basement isn't that small. But you were—'

'I don't like being locked in,' he says before I can get fully into my stride.

'Why, it's not like you went to prison or anything, is it?'

Know your enemy is the Lee family motto and we've done our research on Domingos.

'Prison? What do you think I am?'

'Scrupulously honest, which is pretty impressive for a builder.'

I've always found that strange about him. With his background, I'd expect him to be dodgy, cutting corners and skimming profits. He looks baffled. I'll bet he didn't expect a compliment.

'My father used to lock me in a cupboard whenever he was angry,' he says.

'Was he angry a lot?' I ask replacing one blood-soaked tissue with another on my chin.

'Pretty much all the time.'

'I'm sorry.'

Domingos shrugs, then goes haring up the stairs again as the elevator clanks back into motion. He's making as much noise as he can, but this lift user doesn't notice either. He comes back looking dejected.

'I wonder how many people are still living in this building,' I say. 'There doesn't seem to be much coming and going.'

'Sixty three,' Domingos says.

'Wow, you looked into that much detail on the property?'

'Of course. If you haven't, you're not as serious about this building as I thought.'

'Actually, I was just avoiding a blind date.'

He looks at me blankly and says, as if trying to work something out, 'Is this like Tinder or something? I thought you only hook up with people you like. So why avoid the date?'

'Because I've got Parent Tinder. They get to do all the swiping. My father was trying to set me up.'

Still the same blank look.

'Do you date, Domingos?'

'I don't have time for that.'

'Running a business empire is kind of like that. I assumed you and your PA were—' He's shaking his head, so I stop. 'What were you going to do this evening?'

Domingos gives a sigh. 'I had planned to take that lawyer, Raposo, out to dinner.'

'Wow, I'm surprised you told me that.'

'You already knew I'd most likely do that.'

'Sure, wining and dining is part of the business.'

'Now it looks like we'll be spending the night here.'

We both shudder.

There's a loud bang outside like the front door slamming and Domingos goes running upstairs again to pound on the door. A couple of seconds later, knocking comes from the other side, along with the lawyer's voice. We hear the outer latch being pulled back and yellow light floods in.

'Are you alright?' he asks. 'I couldn't get hold of either of you so I came back.'

Domingos and I explain simultaneously. He gets the gist of it.

'Well, let's get you out of here. Ms Liliana, you look like you should go to the hospital. That's a lot of blood. I hope it wasn't because of the building.'

'It's my own carelessness,' I say, and despite the pain, I'm amused that his lawyerly side is showing.

I'm also wondering how I'm going to get up. That's when Domingos comes down the stairs again, looking considerably more relaxed now that he's no longer locked in, but only after ordering the lawyer to stay by the door and keep it open.

'I will get you up the stairs,' he says. 'If you're okay with me carrying you.'

'Oh no... I couldn't possibly... I'm far too heavy.'

'Not heavier than a stack of bricks,' Domingos says as he slips his arms under me and lifts me as if I weigh nothing.

My heart is pounding, and I feel embarrassed all over again. I also feel like I've just slipped into one of my favourite Chinese dramas while I'm princess carried up the stairs. I expect to be put down in the foyer.

Instead Domingos says, 'Don't worry about us, Mr Raposo, I'll get Liliana to the hospital.'

'Don't be ridiculous,' I say and wriggle about to get out of his arms. 'I can get myself to the hospital, although I really don't think it's necessary.'

'Mmm,' Domingos says, in his usual quiet way that used to annoy me, but today I find oddly reassuring. 'But, you know, I think your chin might need stitches.'

'No!' I wail. 'You should have told me earlier.'

Domingos uses the opportunity to say goodbye to Raposo, walks out of the building and hails a taxi. It's night now and there's a chilly wind.

As he gently lowers me into the back seat, I say, at my fiercest, 'I can do the rest on my own.'

'How are you going to get out of the taxi and into the hospital? I'm going with you.'

'If you get into this taxi, I'm warning you, I'll force you to marry me. You're being far too forward.'

Domingos looks astonished for a moment, then bursts out laughing as he slides in beside me.

'Do you think your father would be happy with me as a son-in-law?'

I'm surprised because he just might be.

'You don't even like me.'

'I might have been mistaken about you,' Domingos murmurs as he leans his head back against the seat and stares out at the

Lisbon streets and the brightly twinkling Christmas lights. It feels like he doesn't want me to see his face.

※

My heart is beating as fast as if I've just finished the hardest work day of my life. Stress and exercise can do that, of course, but I know it's not that. Being that close to Liliana Lee was intoxicating. It's not like I hadn't noticed her beauty. That would have been impossible. But holding her so close somehow made her feel warm and soft and very real.

It's a stupid thing to think, I know. Of course she's real, but I've always kept my distance. How could someone like me approach the ice princess? It's laughable.

But our brief encounter in the basement showed me a different side to her. She's a tough cookie but surprisingly easy to talk to and not, as I'd always assumed, judgemental.

I don't want things to go back to the way they were. That's why I stay with her all the way to the hospital and why I'm sitting in the waiting room while Liliana is being treated. I'm wracking my brain to come up with a way to get closer to her.

She reappears, wheeled in by a far too handsome nurse. She's got a large plaster on her chin, her elbow, and her wrist and a tightly-wrapped bandage has replaced my hanky round her ankle.

'Are you alright?'

'Of course,' Liliana says and gives the nurse a warm smile as he hands her a pair of crutches.

'Remember what the doctor said,' the nurse says. 'Keep off your feet for the next three weeks.'

I help Liliana out of the chair and she uses the sticks to hop over to the row of waiting room chairs.

'So, did you get stitches?' I ask once Liliana has thanked the nurse, and he's gone off to help someone else.

'They did something with strips of plaster so that I won't have a scar, or less of one at least,' Liliana says and looks up at me. 'What are you still doing here? Everyone's getting the wrong idea. The nurse thought you were my boyfriend.'

'Do you think,' I say, 'that you'd like to go for dinner?'

'Now? I'm dishevelled, covered in plasters and I can't even put any weight on my ankle and now you're asking me out?'

'If I don't do it today, I feel like it will never happen.'

'My parents are on their way to fetch me.'

'How about a coffee, then?'

'Where?'

'There's a vending machine at the entrance.'

'Okay,' Liliana says, and she's looking amused.

I return with two small black coffees in paper cups.

'Not the most romantic,' Liliana says.

'But we could maybe give it a try, right?'

'Manuel Domingos, I warned you about getting in the taxi with me, and instead of taking it seriously, you not only ignored me, but waited around in the hospital.'

'I'm a bit badly educated.'

Liliana sighs and shakes her head.

'Very well, then. I suppose we are going to have to give this a try.'

15th December

MOM'S RECIPE FOR A HAPPY MARRIAGE

Mom, my older sister Maria, and I are making Bolo Rei, the Christmas bread covered in crystallised fruit like the dense clusters of jewels on a king's crown. Every December we spend a couple of days baking for uncles, aunts, cousins, nephews and nieces. So now the kitchen is pleasantly toasty and smells of sweet baked bread. The warm December sun in slanting in through the window adding to the cosy, magical feel. This is without a doubt one of my favourite traditions.

Although, this year feels different because Maria is about to get married. It's about time. She's been dating Bernardo for seven years and the rest of the family had pretty much given up hope.

If anyone is going to be married in would be Maria though. She's a tall, slim, elfin-like beauty, just like our tall grandfathers. I'm short and dumpy, just like our grandmothers, who barely made it to 5 feet in height.

Maria is also the successful one. She took an administrative course and became Bernardo's executive PA. Now she earns about four times what I do. I'm a seamstress, with my own little atelier and haberdashery called retROSAria, with a painting of appliquéd roses over the Rosa.

I don't think marriage is on the cards for me. It's especially unlikely because my parents are happily married and have been for nearly fifty years. Why might this be a disadvantage, you ask? Well, when you've seen what true happiness is. It's hard to settle for anything less.

'Rosa,' Mom says breaking into my introspection, 'fetch my shoebox please.'

'Ah the shoebox,' Maria says as I head for my parents' bedroom. 'What wonders are we going to behold today?'

This is a tradition amongst us women. Now and then mom will rummage around her shoebox and tell us a story about one of the pieces. The shoebox is now covered in a pretty quilted overcoat I made when the box started getting shabby.

'Today I have something really important,' Mom says as she takes out one item after another. Both our first pairs of shoes, even then Maria was bigger than me, a bundle of school art, two handmade necklaces, one by me, one by Maria. Dad's favourite pipe, the only one he kept after he gave up smoking. Our high school diplomas, our great grandmother's brooch, a tiny crystal and gold perfume bottle, and finally, hidden right at the bottom is a small, leather notebook.

'Now let me see.' Mom thumbs through the pages, holding the book at a distance so she can read her own small script. 'Ah, here it is,' she says and folds the book open on the kitchen table.

Maria's just finished making our coffee and I slice us each a wedge of Bolo rei. I slather mine with butter. Not because it needs it, but for the sheer luxury.

'This.' Mom taps a page with what looks like a list, but with lots of crossing out, writing squashed between lines and arrows towards other bits in the margin. 'This, is my recipe for a happy marriage.'

'Ah,' I say. 'But Mom, Maria's already been living with Bernardo for years. Aren't you a bit late?'

'There is always something to learn, now listen up.'

She takes a sip of coffee, pauses for dramatic effect and starts reading.

'*1. Never be afraid to make the first move, whether it be proposing, changing careers or moving to another country.*

'You girls know I proposed to your father, don't you?'

'We know,' Maria and I chime. As we settle on the comfortable wooden chairs, the checked green cushions also made by yours truly.

'The poor dear would probably still be single if it wasn't for me.

'*2. Hold an honest and frank discussion over every decision. Really listen to each other and weigh each other's opinions.*

'*3. Never hold a grudge. Even if you have an argument and slam out of the room, the next time you meet, return to your normal civil state as if nothing has happened.*'

'I still find that one hard to do, even within our family,' I say, although dad is a living emblem of dropping any unpleasantness as if it never happened. I don't think I'd want to sweep everything under the carpet, but it works for my parents.

'*4. Be willing to change. Life can throw all sorts of opportunities and disasters at you. You have no choice but to adapt. Don't fight it.*'

This is certainly true for my parents who had to flee Mozambique after the revolution and arrived in Portugal as penniless refugees.

'*5. Remember that you chose to have children. It is your duty to support them until they can look after themselves. They will bring you joy and sorrow, but make sure you see them off to their own lives without regrets.*'

'I hope that's true, Mom,' Maria says giving her a warm smile as she picks a piece of emerald green crystallised melon off the top of her bolo rei.

'Of course it is, you know your dad and I are so proud of the two of you. But unlike in our day, marriage doesn't automatically mean you must have children. That is a decision each couple has to make for themselves.'

'I know,' Maria says. 'Bernardo and I have discussed it but the time has never felt right. Maybe now it will.'

'There's no hurry,' Mom says and raises her finger for emphasis as she reads the next line.

'*6. Careers are important for both the husband and the wife. In the best of circumstances you should both do what you love. But make sure you both have things that occupy your minds.*'

'So Maria can't just quit to become a housewife?' I say pretending to look sorry for her.

Maria laughs, there's no way she would give up her job.

'This is really important,' Mom says. 'I've lost count of the numbers of my female friends who went loopy being stuck at home cleaning and looking after the kids.

'*7. Enjoy spending time together. You got married because you liked each other. Why wouldn't you want to spend time together?*'

This is certainly true of my parents. Even now that they're both retired from their university jobs they spend most of each day together, reading in their study, chatting, going through their massive photo archive or just being quiet together while they eat.

'*8. But also have hobbies and friends that don't overlap.*'

'Really?' I say as I cut myself a second slice of cake. 'You do that?'

'Of course. No two people can have identical interests. Having other interests brings new things to talk about, and learn from.

'*9. There are no winners and losers in a marriage. It's a partnership. You both win if you work together.*

'I know comedians often say the way to have a perfect marriage is for the man to always admit he's wrong and apologise, but that's nonsense. For either side. A partner, especially one who's known you for a long time, will know if you are being insincere. That's why communication is so important. Apologising just to have a quiet life, means that something has gone wrong.

'10. *Never be afraid to revise. As you grow you change and different things will be important to you.*

'Well, that's certainly true,' Maria says running her finger over the crossed out and reworked lines. 'You've done that quite a bit.'

'I'm always looking for the perfect formula. I guess that is my ultimate rule.'

'No need for that,' Dad says strolling into the kitchen. He leans down and gives mom a peck on her lips. 'You've always been perfect for me.'

'Aaah,' Maria and I cry in mock revulsion, waving our hands and laughing.

Our parents' marriage has stood the test of time and they have a great partnership. I hope Maria and Bernardo will have the same, and one day, it might just happen for me too.

16th December

AMY & HER BEST FRIEND

We're standing in a line at a fancy pastry shop in Lisbon, freaking Lisbon! I keep looking up at Jake to check that this is real and that I am actually standing next to him. I want to poke him, just to be doubly sure, but can't think how I'd explain what I was doing so I just shuffle closer to feel his warmth. It's totally surreal, blending into the warm sunshine and the incongruous Christmas decorations covered in artificial snow.

How did I even get here?

Jake and I grew up together in nowheresville, Ohio. Our mothers were neighbors, pregnant together and went into labor on the same day. No kidding.

Jake's older than me by 24 hours, though. The parents always said that reflected our personalities. Jake's bright, always on the go, always looking for a new adventure, an eager beaver and born in under two hours. I'm shy, introverted and super cautious. My mom still rags on me about her epic 26 hours of labor. That was me: afraid to emerge into the world.

So it's no wonder we grew up together, went to the same schools, played and ate at each other's houses and got mistaken for siblings all the time. When we were kids, at least. Until our teens, we were pretty much the same height and the same build.

Then Jake had that teenage growing spurt, and I didn't. He got blonder, cuter and all the girl's attention. My light hair grew darker and I became plainer and even less memorable. He was on the track and field team and the debate team. I was in the computer club and got a sick note as often as I could for sports.

Despite all that, we remained friends, biking to and from school together and then driving when Jake got his first car. Less so when he got his first girlfriend, but I kind of didn't mind. I was Jake's best friend and he would always be there if I needed him.

As the number of girlfriends increased, along with the breakups and the heartbreak, I was the one he'd come to for consolation. I guess he could say things to me he couldn't to his guy friends.

It felt like nothing would ever change. We applied to the same colleges, same first, second and third choices. Different subjects. Computer programming for me, marketing for him.

He got into a place on the east coast, me on the west. I was in denial and went into shock the day he left. I cried for a week. Mostly in the car on the way to college. Mom drove me up and compared the two-day ride to giving birth to me all over again.

Worse was to come. We'd kept in touch, of course, texting every day and getting together at home for the holidays. But when I started talking about jobs and suggested we could work in the same city, he let off a bombshell.

'Amy, I'm moving to Portugal.'

'What? Are you kidding me? Why Portugal? It's bad enough having an entire continent between us, but adding an ocean is too cruel. Don't go, Jake, please don't go.'

Jake, being Jake, laughed and said, 'Why don't you come with? Think of the amazing things we'll see. It's a whole new world, not just Portugal, but it will be super easy to explore the rest of Europe from there.'

I couldn't imagine how I'd do that. So I didn't, and I ugly cried again at the airport, blubbering tears and snot, my face red and blotchy.

'How can you leave with only a backpack? Don't you need a container's worth of supplies to move to another continent?'

'Amy, Amy,' Jake said, wrapping me in a gentle embrace, 'I'll be fine. You have to take care of yourself too, and send me all the gossip.'

I felt hollow after that, like I'd lost way more than just a friend.

Predictably, I got a job in my hometown and told Jake about the changing Fall colors, Mrs. Henry's cat having kittens, again, and the factory closing.

Jake sent me photos of cobbled lanes, brightly colored tiled buildings, exotic cellars with Fado singers, jugs of wine, markets and panoramic views of a city that looked so alien it hardly seemed to be on the same planet.

Then one day I got this text: *Amy, come join me. Come to Portugal!*

Yeah, funny, I texted back.

I'm not joking. There's a job that's perfect for you at my company, Treze.

I had to put my head between my knees and breathe. My heart jumping between breakdancing and flat-lining, my hands shaking, my brain blank. But, because it was Jake, I applied, got the job, packed up everything I owned and went.

Jake met me at the airport with the biggest grin I've ever seen on his face. He seemed taller, broader, more grown up, less attainable. Oh God, what if he had a Portuguese girlfriend? Why did that bother me now, when his girlfriends hadn't troubled me before?

'Amy!' His voice was still the same, still warm and caring. His eyes glowed as he grabbed me in a tight hug. 'God, I've missed you.'

'Not more than I've missed you.' It thrilled me that he kept an arm about me as he relieved me of my luggage and guided me to his car.

He drove me to his place to drop my bags and, despite complaining of jet lag, dragged me out into the sunshine and this line.

'So let me get this straight,' I say, blinking against the glare bouncing off the white cobbles. 'We're going to stand in a line with a one hour wait to get some pastry that you can buy in pretty much every other bakery and cafe in this city.'

'It will be worth it,' Jake says. 'This is the bakery that first created the pastel da nata.'

'Jake, it's a custard tart,' I say with a helpless laugh.

I can't drag my eyes off his face. He looks even more handsome standing here than in all his glamorous selfies.

'Wait and see. In the meantime, tell me about home. How is everyone?'

'Oh, you know, nothing ever changes there, although you should have seen everybody's faces when I told them I was also going to Portugal. Mom literally dropped a plate. I'm not sure she'll ever get the mac and cheese out of the carpet.'

It feels like a dream to be standing next to Jake again, chatting like we've never been apart. Everyone else thinks I'm really quiet. Jake always used to laugh when he heard that.

Time passes so fast I'm surprised when the server clears his throat to get our attention, then leads us through a warren of blue and white tiled corridors and little rooms to our table. It's small and round and Jake is so close — his eyes twinkling. He looks as excited as I feel.

He shows off his Portuguese when he orders and the server is gone and back in a flash, laden with lattes and a plate of half a dozen golden custard tarts nestling in flaky pastry. There are two shakers.

'One's powdered sugar, the other's cinnamon,' Jake says. 'The pastries are pretty sweet, so I usually only go for the cinnamon.'

I follow his lead and cover my tart with a liberal powdering of my favorite spice. The smell of eggy custard and cinnamon is intoxicating. I bite into the tart and my teeth break through the crisp, savory pastry and then the soft, still warm, ridiculously rich custard filling.

'Good lord, it's delicious!'

'Worth it?' Jake asked, tilting his head to the side.

I close my eyes as I take a second bite, focusing on the sweetness and the creaminess.

'So worth it.'

'Good enough to marry me?'

I cough, sending up a cloud of cinnamon that flies up my nose and triggers a sneezing fit and more billowing cinnamon.

Jake laughs and I pull napkin after napkin out of the little metal dispenser, blow my nose, wipe my watering eyes and dust the cinnamon off my cheeks and chin.

'That's a weird joke.'

'I'm not joking,' Jake says. 'I don't think I can live without you.'

Handsome, popular, athletic Jake can't live without me? I realize that I love him too, but I just always knew it would be one-sided. Only, suddenly, it isn't.

'Are you sure?' I have to check because this feels more like wish fulfillment than something that's really happening.

'My cautious Amy,' Jake says with a fond grin as he takes my hand and gives it a squeeze. 'I made a bet with myself that if you came to Portugal, I could be pretty sure you loved me.'

'I do,' I say.

'Good.'

Jake leans over the table and kisses me. It tastes like cinnamon.

17th December

MARQUÊS AND THE CONCERT

They pour into my private box, looking excited. They should be. I've got the royal box at the National Theatre of São Carlos, all baroque gold and red velvet curtains. As ever, Eddy Zeller has arrived with a new woman. More surprising is that this elegant blonde looks younger than his usual choice. He also seems more enamoured by her that with most of his girlfriends.

'I'm Alice Giralt,' she says, as she gives me the usual kiss to either cheek.

'Of The Giralt's?' I ask, because that would be quite a catch even for a Zeller.

'Yeah,' she says with a wry smile.

I guess she's bored with being recognised. But I can't say more as Ragno is looming behind her. As he steps inside he fills the space, making it feel cramped. Unusually for him, he's also arrived with a girlfriend. She's quite pretty but not stunning and seems on the quiet side.

'This is Vanessa,' he says, grinning at her as if they're sharing a secret. 'And this is Rosa de Gouveia. The sister of my soon to be sister-in-law,' Ragno says of a short girl with dark curly hair that makes her look like a doll.

I'm doubly surprised. Ragno and his brother Bernardo rarely get on, so I didn't expect him to take anyone from that side of his family under his wing.

'And this,' Ragno says, turning to the two women, 'is Marquês.'

'Marquês?' they both say, and look surprised.

'It's a nickname,' I say, because if I don't jump in, Ragno and Eddy are liable to make a big mystery out of it and tease both me and the women.

'It's not only a nickname,' Eddy says as he heads to the back of the box to examine the spread of food I've laid on. 'His family are nobility. You just have to take one look at his tall stature and stately visage to know that.'

Eddy is joking. He's right that I'm tall and, I am told, handsome, but it has more to do with my father and grandfather marrying models than with the family genes. These had produced some terrifyingly deformed ancestors before the family started marrying out.

'And his names tells you the rest,' Ragno weighs in.

These two have been doing this routine since we were in high school.

'You need a whole page with all your names, don't you, my friend?' Ragno says, patting my shoulder. 'While I have a mere twelve and that's painful enough when it comes to filling in official forms.'

'A whole page? I'm the same as Ragno. I also only have twelve,' Alice says and laughs. 'Only! I don't get to say that often.'

'I have a mere eight,' Eddy says, and Vanessa and Rosa confess to only having seven between them. 'There you go. It proves he's nobility.'

'But do you like being called Marquês?' Rosa asks, and she has to tilt her head back to look up at my face.

'It's better than my name.'

'You have so many to choose from,' Eddy says. 'You don't have to go with the first one.'

'None of them are good.'

'Really?' Rosa asks but looks surprised, possibly by my lack of originality, which makes me want to justify myself.

'Well... I am Ildegardo Lisbano Vagner Hilarião etc, etc, etc with similar old-fashioned names all the way to my surname: Quintanilha e Vargas.'

'Ildegardo,' Eddy says with the same chuckle he used in high school.

'Enough,' I say, and hold up my hand. 'Get some food, the concert is about to start.'

We're here to listen to Céu, one of the most popular singers in Portugal, with a sizeable following around the world. She usually plays packed stadiums, but she's also doing this Christmas special.

Naturally, the lovers pair off and I land up next to Rosa de Gouveia, who gives me a sympathetically friendly smile that seems to imply singletons should stick together, but nothing more. Then, as the lights go down, she switches all her attention to the stage.

What with one thing and another, I'm used to women making moves on me, so I'm a bit taken aback at being dismissed. I find myself looking down at Rosa quite a few times during the concert. She has a very expressive face and as she's drawn into the music, a blend of Fado, samba and rock, she bops about in her seat. I get the feeling that she'd be up and dancing if she only had the space.

The concert ends after two hours and applause erupts. Rosa leaps to her feet, calling encore, encore, along with most of the crowd, and they perform two more songs before Céu bows and leaves the stage for the last time.

Rosa sighs rapturously and leans back in the chair with a broad smile on her face. It's the relaxed position of a woman without a care in the world. I'm more used to women being deliberately elegant and cool. Showing off how perfect they could be for me.

'Looks like you enjoyed that.'

Rosa tilts her head so she can see my face and grins at me, which makes her nose crinkle in a charming way.

'That was amazing! I'm glad I came.'

'It surprised me to see you with Ragno.'

'Yeah,' Rosa leans forward to look past me to the end of our row, where Ragno is chatting to his date. 'I was surprised, too. The only other time I've met Ragno was at Maria and Bernardo's engagement announcement.'

'I think you may have been invited in a misguided attempt at pairing us up,' I say. It's the only reason I could think of. 'But I'm not—'

I stop because Rosa giggles, a deep full body laugh all the way from her belly, not something sweet and tittering like I'm used to.

She leans towards me, closer than expected and whispers, 'I'm here to make his date more comfortable.'

'I beg your pardon?'

'She's ordinary, like me. I don't think Ragno knows many poor people.'

It's a surprising reason that I want to explore, but everyone else has got up now to chat and help themselves to more food. Rosa hurries over to the spread and starts piling her plate to the brim. The other two women are being more circumspect and restrict themselves to two or three little morsels. I help myself to a few choice slices of cheese and smoked ham while I gaze out into the crowd that is slowly filing its way out of the theatre, their faces glowing as they reminisce over the concert.

At that moment, the door to the box swings open and Céu steps inside. She's everything you'd expect from a celebrity. She's tall, beautiful and eccentric. She's changed from her skimpy stage costume, all diamantés and feathers, and is now in a figure-hugging blue velvet dress that matches her ombre blue hair, which fades to white at the roots.

'Marquês,' she says in her deep melodic voice as she envelops me in a hug and gives me a kiss on each cheek. In her monstrous platform shoes, she's a touch taller than me.

'Céu,' I say as I step out of the embrace. 'A magnificent performance, as always. Let me introduce you to my friends.'

I do the rounds, starting with Alice who's closest and ending at Rosa, who's put down her plate and is staring up at Céu with the unabashed adoring gaze of a fan. She steps forward to say hello and comes over all shy, stuttering and blushing so deeply her face looks like a shining red sun.

'It was a fantastic performance,' Ragno says. 'You get better and better each year.'

'You know Céu?' Rosa whispers to me.

She looks awestruck and her gaze doesn't shift from her idol's face.

'We're cousins,' I say. 'Distant, but family nonetheless.'

'Wow!'

I find it funny that Rosa thinks this is greater than all my own attributes.

'Do you want a picture with her?'

Rosa looks taken aback by the idea, but I apparently rise in her estimation for making the suggestion.

'Would that be possible?'

'Of course.'

I'm playing my best, cool, unflappable self. I'm not used to open enthusiasm and adoration. Everyone else in this room is the same, as if meeting a celebrity is an everyday thing. Does this woman have no sense of how others see her?

'How about some photos?' I say to Céu.

'I'd be happy to,' she says and her manager, a short man in a tight, white satin suit, takes a whole host of pictures for us, each person handing him their phone as we do group shots and pairs.

'Thanks,' I say at the end. 'Would you like to stay for something to eat?'

'I'm too tired, darling,' Céu says. 'I'm off to bed,' and blowing kisses, she leaves.

'She is so cool,' Rosa says while smiling lovingly down at the photo of Céu and her.

'Worth coming?'

'Oh, for sure,' Rosa says and heads back to her abandoned plate of food. 'I would have come just for the concert.'

'Not to meet people?'

Rosa pauses, a croquette halfway to her mouth that she puts back on the plate.

'I enjoy meeting people, of course, but…' she pauses as if trying to work out how best not to offend. 'It's not likely we'll ever meet again, is it?'

I suppose she's right, but I feel like playing devil's advocate.

'Why wouldn't we meet again?'

'Different worlds,' Rosa says and waves the hand not holding her plate to encompass the theatre and our box. 'I know Ragno's family are bankers, and Eddy is a Zeller, and considering your family and what you can spend in a night, I'm guessing you're also filthy rich.'

'I suppose so.'

'What do you do?' Rosa asks, but it's just for form's sake.

I've realised that she feels so far out of my league that she's decided isn't worth making any effort to attract me.

'Wine,' I say. 'My family's fortune, like many a noble, is founded upon land. We own vineyards from the south of Portugal to the north.'

'While I'm just a seamstress.'

'A noble profession.'

Rosa laughs. She seems to find me genuinely funny. I'm not used to that.

'You two are getting on well,' Eddy says and I note he's got his arm around Alice, holding her close. 'Don't let him push you away, Rosa. Marquês is a prickly character. He's always driving women off.'

'Gold diggers,' I say.

'What you need,' Ragno says, 'is a genuine damsel in distress.'

'I've even had women fake that.'

'Emphasis on genuine,' Alice says. 'I would have got washed out to sea if it wasn't for Eddy.'

'And Ragno saved me from humiliation when my boyfriend dumped me at a restaurant,' Vanessa says.

'Well, you guys got lucky,' I say, looking back down at Rosa, who has returned to perusing the food, her fingers hovering over an eclair. 'But I'm being chased all the time.'

'I'm the exact opposite,' Rosa says, unexpectedly, without looking up. 'Nobody likes me.' Then she realises what she's just said and looks up, blushing. 'I mean, potential lovers. I have plenty of friends.'

'Marquês doesn't even have that. He's always pushing people away. He's not called the Ice Prince for nothing,' Eddy says and draws Alice away for a more private canoodle in the corner. Ragno is similarly distracted by his date.

'While I'm more like one of the seven dwarfs,' Rosa says, tilts her head to one side in thought and adds, 'the cute one.'

'I find it hard to believe you've had no offers. Maybe you're not making enough effort. Don't you plan on getting married?'

Rosa gives an infectious, gurgling laugh.

'It's not the Middle Ages, you know? I don't need a man to survive. I have my own apartment and my own business and I make enough money to support myself and take the occasional glamorous overseas trip. I'm fine.'

I just blink at her. I've said the same: I'm fine on my own. But that's because I'm a man, very rich, and never actually meant it. Rosa seems entirely genuine. I want to ask her about it, but there's another tap at the door. The theatre manager has arrived to politely request we vacate.

We walk in silence out of the theatre. Ragno hand in hand with Vanessa, Eddy with his arm around Alice. They both look like they've finally found the right women for them.

I glance down at Rosa, who's landed up walking beside me. She's grown cuter as the night progressed. But I guess this is it. We wave Eddy and Alice off as they climb into a taxi, then I walk with Ragno, Vanessa and Rosa to his car, give them all farewell kisses and head for my car. I feel melancholy that I won't see Rosa again.

I spin around and run back. Rosa is just about in the car, one foot still on the pavement.

'Hey, Rosa,' I shout, 'how about we try it?'

'Try what?' she says, looking confused.

'Dating.'

I grab hold of the car door so Ragno can't pull off. Rosa looks surprised, and I'm wondering what the hell has got into me, and simultaneously how I convince a woman with no expectations or belief in love.

'You and me?' she says, pointing.

'Who else?'

'Really?'

'Absolutely!'

'Alright,' she says. 'Call me,' and then she pulls the door shut, and the car pulls away.

I'm left standing on the pavement with a stupid grin on my face. I'm pretty sure Rosa doesn't expect to hear from me again. I will definitely call her. I've already planned where I'm going to take her for our first date.

18th December

CATARINA'S CONFESSION

I'm walking down the pedestrianised pink road which looks tacky in the weak afternoon sunshine. It's not helped by the white plastic Christmas lights woven into scrolls, that are ugly in daylight. My sweaty hand grips the handle of my suitcase so tight it hurts.

What on earth am I doing here? I must have lost my mind. Then again, do I have a choice?

This man, Tómas, who I met once and had a drunken one-night stand with, is suddenly, and unexpectedly, the father of my baby. He's drop dead gorgeous, of course, otherwise I wouldn't have screwed up my courage to throw myself at him.

He owns a nightclub on the Rua do Arsenal, the epicentre of Lisbon night life, and women are always hitting on him. I was therefore surprised, and rather pleased, that I grabbed his attention.

I was so embarrassed when I woke up in his bed the following morning, though. So I scrambled into my clothes, muttered an embarrassed apology and made a run for it. I swore I'd never go to his place again, or even go clubbing at all.

I had my studies to keep on top of after all, I planned to become a music teacher and that takes hours of dedication. Not just the studying, but honing my craft. I play the piano and the flute.

Then I discovered I was pregnant and got myself kicked out of the house. Dad is old-fashioned that way. First, he demanded that I tell him who the father was so he could make him take responsibility. He'd assumed I'd been taken advantage of. But, drunken haze excepted, I knew exactly what I was doing. And, although the consequences are stunning, there's no way I'm getting rid of the baby.

I had always planned to have a family, I just hadn't expected it to arrive so abruptly. I mean, I'm one of the more cautious of my group, and aside from some fumbling experiments with a high school sweetheart I haven't really even done anything. Until the night at the club where personal attraction, alcohol fuelled bravado and the encouragement of my friends, drove me to this situation.

I stop in front of the club and gather my courage. A gang of six burly men are unloading crates of alcohol. It looks like I'll have to go through them to get to the door. It's enough to make me turn away, but then I remember I have nowhere else I can go.

I'm still dithering when he steps out of the club and a wave of nausea washes over me. Tómas goes up to the truck to hoist a crate of beers, then on his way back in, he notices me.

'Can I help you?' he asks, his gaze going from my face to my suitcase and back to my face.

'Um... I don't know if you remember me, I'm Catarina,' I say so softly I can't even hear my own voice over the bang and clank of the bottle bearing labourers.

How could he remember a girl from six weeks ago when he has women throwing themselves at him every night? I have no illusions that I'm memorable and the only one to ever share his bed.

He comes closer and says, 'Speak up, I'm busy.'

'You probably don't remember me, but—'

'Of course I remember you,' he says, much to my surprise. 'You're the girl who ran off before I could offer you breakfast.'

'Ah,' I say.

So not a good memory for him.

'But what has that to do with you being here now?'

I'd rehearsed this conversation over and over, in the metro, then the tram, then the short walk down the road. I'd imagined all sorts of questions and crafted carefully phrased responses designed to soften the blow.

'I'm pregnant,' I blurt out.

He drops the crate, bottles shatter and beer spatters everywhere. 'You're what?'

Tómas steps around the frothing crate, grabs my elbow, and pulls me further out into the road.

'I'm pregnant.'

I'm stuck in this rut, unable to think of anything else to say now that he's glaring down at me. He has green eyes. I never noticed that in the dark of the club and the dimness of his room.

'Is it mine?'

It's a fair question and one I have prepared for.

'You're the only one I—'

'So what do you want me to do about it?'

His expression is hard and angry as I expected. My father's face looked much the same, but also mixed with disgust.

'I... I just need somewhere to stay for a while. I... I don't want anything else. It's just a bit sudden. My father threw me out and none of my friends are around and I don't have money for a hotel so...' I stare helplessly up at him.

Will he believe that he really is my last resort? I have honestly tried everyone else I know, but for one or other excellent reason, none of them can put me up.

'Your father?' Tómas asks, leaning even closer to examine my face. 'You told me you're an adult.'

I'm surprised at his good memory and say, 'I am.'

'Then why are you still relying on your parents?'

'I'm in my final year at university and it's cheaper to live at home.'

I'm shaking and I hope he can't see that. It might be useful, but it makes me feel pathetic. He glares down at me, his brow deeply wrinkled, but at least it looks like he's giving this some thought. I wonder whether this kind of thing has ever happened to him before. It must have, right? Then I wonder what he did about it.

He sighs and says, 'You'd better come inside.'

I follow him, past the dropped crate of beers where foam is still creeping through the shattered glass, past the others who've gone back to unloading the truck, through the dark nightclub that smells of stale alcohol and too many people, past the pair of cleaners who stop their low voiced conversation, and start swishing their mops about the pale marble floor, and through the black swinging door with the big metal letters saying PRIVATE.

I've been this way before, in an excited drunken state, all the way to the top floor and Tómas's apartment. As we reach the steps, he takes the suitcase out of my hand. He folds in the handle and starts up the stairs, carrying it for me. I'm so grateful I could cry. I wouldn't have blamed him if he'd just left me to do everything myself.

'Come in,' he says and waves me in the general direction of his sofa.

The apartment is surprisingly light in daytime, large and open plan. I'm embarrassed that I remember so little of it. Then my eyes alight on the bed and I feel myself blushing. So I hastily look away and perch on the sofa, my back to the bed.

Tómas puts the suitcase down next to the sofa and leans down to examine my face again.

'You look very pale.'

'Do I?'

I'm not sure what my response should be.

'Mmm,' he says and wanders over to the other end of his apartment, where a long bar makes up his kitchen.

Tómas takes down two coffee cups, pauses, gives me another thoughtful look, sets the coffee machine going for one cup, goes to his fridge and pours a glass of milk. He brings the milk and coffee over, and sits opposite me on the edge of a brown leather club chair. He's so calm that this can't be the first time he's done this.

'When did you find out?'

'A week ago.'

I don't even try to pick up the milk. My hands are still shaking so much I'll just spill.

'And when did you tell your father?' Tómas asks, watching me over the lip of the coffee cup as he takes a sip.

'This morning.'

'I see.'

'I've been looking for somewhere else to go since then. I swear you weren't my first choice.'

Tómas glances at the chunky watch on his wrist.

'Have you eaten anything today?'

I shake my head.

'No wonder you're so pale and shaky.' He downs his coffee and heads back to the kitchen area. 'Is there anything you can't eat?'

I shake my head again. I'm not sure I can eat right now, but I'm grateful Tómas is being so calm. I'd feared a big scene like at home. My dad slapped me and called me a slut and my mother was crying and held onto his arm to buy me the time to fling some clothes into a suitcase before my father pushed me out of the house.

I pray he isn't just going to feed me and send me on my way again. I also dread what he might have to say about the baby. Right now he looks absorbed in cutting a bread roll in two and filling it with cheese and ham.

'Come,' he says and puts the sandwich on his dining room table. 'Eat, then we'll talk.'

I sit down at the table. The scrape of the dining room chair makes me cringe because I've been clumsily loud.

'Um... do you mind if we talk first?' I say, gathering my courage. 'I'm too scared to be able to eat.'

Tómas purses his lips and slowly blows out his breath. Maybe he isn't as relaxed as I'd assumed.

'I honestly don't know what to do. This is all rather sudden, but I assume you have some thoughts on the matter, so let's hear them.'

'I'm going to keep the baby,' I say, glaring defiantly at him even though my pulse is drumming in my ears from fright.

'Do you have any money? Or a job?'

'I can find something. I would have liked to finish my degree, but I guess that won't be possible now.'

'Are you sure your father won't take you back? It must have come as a shock to him, too. Maybe when he calms down—'

'There is no way he'll change his mind. And if it wasn't for him paying for my education, I would already have left. We don't have a great relationship.'

'I see.'

Tómas gazes at the table top as if it might have different answers.

'What did you do before?' I ask.

'Before what?'

'Before... when some other woman got pregnant.'

He blinks at me, as if he doesn't understand, and then his eyebrows go up.

'You have the wrong idea about me. Just because I own a nightclub and plenty of women throw themselves at me, doesn't mean that I bed a different woman every night. Or have faced this situation before.'

'Really?'

I feel comforted to hear it. Like we're suddenly in the same boat. Well, not quite. Once I sort myself out, he'll be free to continue his life as before.

'You seemed genuinely nice,' Tómas says quite gently.

'Sorry.' I'm embarrassed all over again. 'But I won't be a burden to you for long. And I won't expect you to look after the baby either.'

'Why not?'

'What?'

'It takes two to make a baby, doesn't it? Why do you feel that I should be shielded from this burden?'

I must look like an astonished guppy as I stare at him. I'd expected denial, I'd expected to be pushed out and cursed at and told to know my place. This... this is totally not what I expected.

'Well... yes. I suppose so.'

'Look, I won't tell you I'm thrilled. This news has come as a shock. But, just because I have the convenient distance of not having a child growing inside me, doesn't mean that I get to wash my hands of it.'

'Millions would disagree,' I say, looking down at my as yet untouched sandwich. 'Are you... maybe the son of a single parent or something?'

Tómas laughs and says, 'No, but I do have an arsehole dad.'

'Oh,' I say and find myself able to smile. This hasn't gone as badly as I feared. Then another horrible thought occurs. 'You don't have a girlfriend, do you?'

'No girlfriend,' Tómas says. 'I'm too busy to have a meaningful relationship.'

'Oh.' Maybe that explains the willingness for a one-night stand. Then again, maybe that was just me. After all, he was going to offer me breakfast. Maybe he hadn't been taking things as lightly as I'd assumed. 'So... what now?'

Again that disconcerted puffing out of air.

'I suppose we need to take it one day at a time. I'll sort out somewhere for you to stay.'

'Not here?' I ask, surprised by how disappointed I feel.

Tómas has grown to heroic proportions in my mind. It's foolish of me. After all, he's right about the responsibility side of things. I had just expected the opposite of what I'm getting.

'I do mean here. The open plan makes it tricky to create a private space, but I'll sort something out,' Tómas says.

Unexpected tears flood down my face, dripping off my chin. I wipe at them with my fingers but a pent up damn of terrified what-ifs has burst. I'm trying not to sob out loud and make pathetic little hics.

'Hey now, don't cry,' Tómas says and hurries around the table. He pats my shoulder somewhat uncertainly, and then wraps an arm around me and gently pulls me closer. 'It's been tough, so far, hasn't it?'

I bury my face in his sweater so he can't see it and just nod.

'But it's okay now, right? We can get through this together.'

His words make me want to bawl even louder, but from heart shaking relief. I don't have to do this alone. My baby and I have found a safe haven.

19th December

GENARO'S CHRISTMAS PARTY

'How did it go?' Andrews asks as he emerges from his operating room at the same time as I leave mine.

'No problem. How about you?'

'Same,' he says. 'Now I'm going to take a 20 minute power nap in my office then I'll get ready for the party.'

'Ah yes, the party.'

'You forgot, didn't you?' Andrews says, still grinning, but this one because he thinks he's caught me out.

'This year, I remembered.' I have actually never forgotten. I've just pretended so I could avoid the event. 'This year, I've got a partner.'

'You've got a girlfriend?'

Andrews looks astonished. I've known him a long time. Ever since my residency. He's an English doctor but moved to Lisbon years ago, he claims for health reasons. The gossip is there was more to the story, but I don't care.

Since I've taken too long to answer as I peel off my gloves and wash my hands, he leans forward to examine my face and says, 'You've actually got a girlfriend, Genaro?'

'Partner,' I repeat, mindful of Doroteia's strictures that I may not call her a girlfriend or take it for granted that we will see each other after this date.

'Wow, congratulations,' Andrews says, giving my shoulder a friendly tap, which I don't appreciate. 'I look forward to meeting this wonder woman.'

I nod and head towards my office via the corridors of the hospital, where there is more activity than usual. The nurses and junior doctors always make such a fuss over Christmas. There are cards on all the desks and more flowers and decorations than is appropriate. I was overruled on this years ago too. So now, aside from my domain where it's banned, I say nothing about the hygiene risks of tinsel.

A couple of the younger nurses smile and wave hello as I pass. I ignore them. The older, more experienced women no longer bother throwing themselves at me.

I have tried dating fellow medical professionals. It has never ended well. I inevitably get accused of being disinterested, preoccupied with my work and, occasionally, cruel.

I don't intend to be cruel. But I also don't see why I have to guess what other people are thinking, or attempt to conform to their needs and desires. I have been told this is unnaturally harsh but, as I expect the same attitude towards myself, I believe it is fair.

I would be happy enough remaining single, but there is social pressure to conform. My life would be less irritating if I had a partner to attend events with. It would also put an end to some women trying to make themselves alluring to me. I am not so naïve as to believe it will stop all of them. I have observed other married doctors being stalked and stalking attractive prey. But it would at least give me a reason to decline.

I also believe I can learn from Doroteia. As a writer, she has the skill to explain about appropriate reactions more clearly than my colleagues can. She is also refreshingly direct. She made it clear what she will accept and what she won't without making me jump through verbal and emotional hoops to get there.

In addition, she accepted my initial proposal after giving it proper consideration. There is a good probability that we will achieve a satisfactory relationship in time.

I finish changing from my scrubs into a formal suit and check myself in the mirror. I've been able to give up the crutch, as my knees, though sore, are much improved. The same can't be said for my face, where the double black eyes from the broken nose have faded to a blotched purple and yellow. It can't be helped and as Doroteia has texted to say she's about to arrive, I head for reception.

Doroteia is wearing a black velvet dress with sparkles, long sleeves and a deep scoop neck that emphasises her elegant collarbones.

'You look beautiful,' I say as I walk up to her and give her a kiss on each cheek.

It is what I would normally say as it's expected, but in Doroteia's case, it is true.

'Thank you,' she says, giving me a critical once over. 'You look pretty good yourself.'

I believe her. She isn't the type to sugarcoat things.

'So, this is where you work,' Doroteia says taking it all in with a professional eye.

I suspect some of what she sees may land up in a book one day.

'I've read another of your novels,' I say as I wave her toward the elevators.

'More research or were you just in need of something to put you to sleep?' she asks with a twinkle in her eye.

'Both,' I say, and stand behind her as we enter the lift.

'I assume, as it's a massive hospital that has to run twenty-four hours a day, that you don't have one giant staff party.'

'Correct. The parties are divided by department. We're heading for the surgery department's party.'

'On the roof,' Doroteia says glancing towards the lift button where I'd selected the top floor.

'We have a rooftop terrace and cafeteria. It helps save money for events like this.'

'How practical,' Doroteia says with an amused smile.

There's more to what she's just said, but I can't figure it out and don't have the time either. I usher her out of the lift, placing my left hand lightly against her back. She glances back and gives me a smile, which I take as tacit approval of the gesture.

'Ah, Professor Genaro,' Andrews says, coming up to the two of us, trailing his wife. 'You must introduce me to your partner.'

He gives me a conspiratorial grin to make sure I am aware that he has deliberately said partner.

'This is Doroteia,' I say, 'and this is Mr Andrews, our second best surgeon and his wife, Fiona.'

Fiona gives Doroteia a vaguely alarmed look before leaning forward for a greeting. She's been in the country for nearly two decades but barely gets by with her Portuguese. She also used to be a paediatric nurse and has an infantile manner I find disconcerting in a middle-aged woman.

'Nice to meet you,' Doroteia say switching effortlessly to English.

I add this to her list of impeccable qualities.

Andrews launches into a dissection of our latest joint operation and Doroteia and Fiona drift towards the lavish buffet. It's been prepared by the cooks from the staff canteen who always lay on a superb spread when they cater for parties.

'She's not bad,' Andrews says once he judges they're far enough away to not hear.

'She's beautiful.'

'Well, I'm glad you think so.'

'It's an objective fact.'

'Beauty is usually in the eye of the beholder.'

'Although there are certain attributes that are universally acknowledged and Doroteia has them; almost perfect facial symmetry, a small nose and large brown eyes with long lashes.'

'Do you know,' Andrews says, looking up at me with a thoughtful expression. 'I think you really like her.'

I nod.

'I have wondered whether I am suffering from a case of erotic transference.'

'Because she saved you from the crash?'

'Exactly, but I believe it is more than that. She is an admirable individual.'

'One who may need rescuing. The pack of envy is heading her way.'

'The what?' I ask, looking in the same direction as Andrews.

'All the nurses and junior doctors who were after you. They will do their utmost to drive her off. A similar pack has a go at Fiona every time we attend a party together. You'd think after our twenty years of marriage those predators would realise they're wasting their time, but no.'

'Then I'd best deal with the situation,' I say and head towards Doroteia.

Fiona makes an escape as the pack closes around Doroteia. I can break it up with a single word, but I'm curious to see what happens, so I lurk within hearing distance and peek around the Christmas tree.

'I can't believe Professor Genaro came with a date today,' the head nurse of my surgery team says and looks Doroteia up and down in an insulting way. 'What is it you do again? Writer wasn't it?'

'That's right.'

Doroteia sounds perfectly calm.

'I hear it doesn't pay well.'

'I manage.'

'But not so well, obviously,' one of the junior doctors says in a sweetly sarcastic tone. 'Your dress looks second hand. I'll bet I'm already earning more than you.'

'Genaro doesn't seem to mind.'

The whole group gasps.

'What?' Doroteia asks. 'Did I say something wrong?'

'You just call him by his first name?'

I hadn't actually noticed this fact, which amuses me.

'Why shouldn't I?' Doroteia asks. 'It's his name, isn't it?'

'Well, yes, but Professor Genaro never lets anyone drop his title. He once had a nurse fired because of it.'

'Mmm. It makes sense in a work context. When you have life or death situations, a clear decision-making hierarchy is critical.'

She got that right too. She really is an impressive woman.

'But what can you do for him?' my head nurse asks. 'You will be no use in helping forward his career.'

'I have absolutely no intention of helping his career. He's more than capable of doing that himself,' Doroteia says. 'And I have no expectations of him forwarding mine. Why should he?'

'Everyone knows connections in the medical world are a key to success.'

'Well, then he'd have to go out with another top surgeon or hospital director, wouldn't he?'

Doroteia has just told all the women surrounding her exactly why they were never in the running in the first place, and it has nothing to do with their status. I step out from behind the tree so that I am now in Doroteia's line of sight. She gives me a bright smile and steps past the pack, her hand outstretched.

'Fancy a dance?' she says.

I take her hand and, after giving the pack a black look, lead Doroteia towards the dance floor.

'I'm not actually a good dancer,' I say. 'But I am a fast learner.'

'That's alright,' Doroteia says and veers away from the dance floor to a shrubby, quieter nook.

I'm relieved to see that she looks amused

'I'm sorry about the ambush. I wasn't aware such things happen as I've never brought a date before.'

'I won't say it wasn't stressful, but it was also fascinating.'

Doroteia intercepts a passing waiter and helps herself to one of his glasses of champagne.

'Fascinating?'

'I was very lucky that I was never bullied at school. And as I work from home, I've never been bullied in the workplace. So to experience it so blatantly, but in a low-risk way, was useful.'

'You're going to put it in a book?'

'Let's say it might make any future bullying scenes I write sound more authentic.'

'I won't allow you to be subjected to such a thing again.'

'The only way to do that is to never invite me out again,' Doroteia says looking up at me over the rim of her glass as she takes an elegant sip.

It sounds like a challenge.

'I could order them not to do anything to you.'

'You can't be everywhere to ensure that they comply, for instance, the ladies' loos.'

'You could tell me about it and I'd discipline them.'

'Don't be silly. I can look after myself. So I assume that means you would like to go on another date?'

'You said you have a book launch in the new year.'

'I did, didn't I?'

'If I passed your test this evening. So, are you enjoying yourself?'

'Are you?'

'I have never enjoyed staff events. But it is more tolerable with your company.'

'I'm the same. They aren't really my cup of tea,' Doroteia says, 'so, how about we slip away and go do our own thing?'

'Our own thing like what? Since it's so near Christmas, all the restaurants will be fully booked.'

'I wasn't thinking about food.'

Doroteia steps up to me, tilts her head back and closes her eyes.

'Ah,' I say and lean in for a kiss. 'Your place or mine?'

20th December

HOMERO'S DISCOVERY

I 'm feeling conspicuous at this wedding and that isn't like me. I'm used to being the lord of all I survey but today's crowd barely seem to notice me. Hundreds of people have filled the largest ballroom of the Ocean Breeze Hotel. It's glittering with massive arrangements of white chrysanthemums whose pungent leafy scent mixes with the perfumes of all the women and some of the men. I can't complain about that. Perfume is my business.

But the combination of scents bothers me. Not as much as it must surely be bothering my eldest son, Armando, but bad enough. It's making me irritable.

Or maybe that's because I came alone or because most of the guests are a generation younger than me. I glance at my watch, deciding it's time to leave when I catch sight of an old foe.

Agata Alte, seated beside an enormous white and silver Christmas tree in one of the high backed velvet chairs with an ornate gold frame, looking every inch an empress. Her hair has turned completely white and is styled in waves reminiscent of an old time movie star.

She's probably here for the same reason as I am: networking amongst the upper echelons of Portuguese society. She's the grand dame of the hotel industry and her grandson and heir is probably somewhere in this crowded banquet hall of her flagship hotel.

Her grandson is a couple of years younger than my eldest son. She fell pregnant scandalously young, and her son also got married early. It's all water under the bridge now.

I settle on the second chair grouped around the low coffee table.

'Hello, Agata,' I say.

She looks me up and down as if I'm as unimportant as a waiter before giving me a gracious slow nod.

'Well, well, Homero Zeller. How are you?'

'Bored.'

'You'd have to be to come and talk to me.'

'Is your grandson about?'

'He couldn't come. I'm deputising. How about your family?'

Her question is just for form's sake. The only interest Agata has in my family is how much money she can make from them.

'Well, Armando was the best man. Bernardo is his friend after all. And Diana's baby is due soon. Eddy is dating a Giralt so he's also doing well.'

I say nothing about my daughter, Elena, who has turned up to the wedding with her PA. She's still sulking about Armando getting the CEO role and no amount of evidence that he's the best choice for the job will convince her.

'How about César?'

'Still single,' Agata says. Her tone implies that this is an irritation for her. As her sole surviving heir she's probably worried on both personal and business fronts. 'I heard you're single again too.'

I expected the dig. In fact I'm surprised Agata waited as long as she did before saying something.

'Your wife went off with... was it her tennis coach? And 20 years her junior too. Good for her.'

'So you think she did well, do you?'

'Come now, Homero, don't pretend you were faithful to her during your marriage. She was the second as well, wasn't she? A younger model to replace your first wife. It's amusing that you didn't expect the same thing to happen to you.'

I've heard similar unflattering comments from Elena and my first wife and I might have stormed off at this point but for two reasons. One, I would never give Agata the satisfaction, and, two a waiter has bent towards us, tray in hand, offering drinks. I take a red wine, Agata chooses champagne.

'I'm surprised you didn't bring some pretty young thing to this event too.'

I had considered it, but in the end decided against it. I also don't bother asking Agata about whether she has a date. There's no need. She's never been seen with a man after her husband died in the accident that also took her son and daughter-in-law.

I take a deep sip of wine and watch the energetic bright chatter of the wedding guests.

'They're a different breed from us,' I say and an unexpected sigh escapes me.

'More international, more open minded and much less interested in obeying their elders.'

'That's for sure. I would never have dared go against the path my father laid out for me. There was no question of me not taking over the family business.'

'Filial obedience no longer exists,' Agata says and takes a sip of champagne. 'To them we are the villains if we try to guide them.'

I laugh, I'm pretty sure Agata's guidance sounds like an absolute order to her grandson.

'Maybe having a young girlfriend helps keep you current. I suppose that is one advantage.'

'Honestly, I never considered that.'

'No, well, that's probably not why old men like to bed nubile young women, I suppose,' Agata says.

I tilt my head to give her a closer look. Considering her age she's remarkably well maintained with a slim figure and clear skin. Then I shudder. She's too terrifying.

'Why did you never remarry?'

'I didn't have the time and in the end I didn't want to. I became the boss and I like being in charge.'

'It was a massive role to take over at an extremely stressful time.'

Now Agata tilts her head to examine me.

'Are you actually giving me sympathy? If so, you're twenty years too late.'

'We never saw eye to eye on anything, did we?'

'Probably not.'

'But now, ironically, I feel closer to you than to anyone else in this room.'

Agata laughs. It is deep and surprisingly alluring. I'm curious about what she found so amusing for the first time since we've known each other but two young men have just arrived accompanied by their dates.

Agata stands up to give the young men a kiss to each cheek and be introduced to their partners.

'Agata, this is Vanessa,' Ragno Oldenbourg, the gigantic youngest brother of the groom says waving at a slim but to my eyes plain young woman who is dwarfed by her date.

'It's lovely to meet you,' Agata says and turns to the second couple. 'And you, Marquês?'

This tall slim young man dwarfs his date too, but more because she's probably the shortest woman here.

'Rosa de Gouveia,' Marquês says of his diminutive date.

'Ah, any relation to the bride?' Agata asks as she leans down to greet the young woman.

'She's my sister,' Rosa says with a sunny smile that explains why Marquês, a usually rather withdrawn young man, is attracted to her.

'Well then perhaps we will be planning your wedding next,' Agata says.

'We'd get married on my estate,' Marquês says in his abrupt way that usually sets people's backs up.

'We've only just started dating,' Rosa says blushing and giving Marquês a fierce look.

'Well there's no hurry, now go off and enjoy yourself,' Agata says as she resumes her seat. 'No need to be hanging around old fogeys like us.'

The couples issue polite denials, but accept their dismissal.

'Can you believe those two are actually talking to each other?' Ragno says overly loudly as they leave. 'I've got to tell Eddy.'

'It seems even we are fodder for gossip,' Agata says.

I'm struck by her serenity and elegance and wonder why I've not noticed it before.

'Why have we never got on?'

Agata turns in her seat to look me up and down.

'You've made no secret of your disdain for me over the years. I assumed because you were a hypocritical man who believed he could do whatever he wanted with young women, but that young women couldn't behave in the same way.'

'Maybe it's just because of your direct way of speaking. You've never held back, Agata.'

'Neither have you.'

I realise it's true, and some of what I've said about Agata, sometimes to her face, sometimes not, has been on the hypocritical side.

'I am sorry about that.'

Agata looks astonished.

'What has happened to you, Homero? Have you been diagnosed with cancer or something?'

'What?' I say, equally surprised. 'No, I'm fine.'

'Well, you sound like a man going around making amends. It's very out of character.'

'Maybe because I am about to become a grandfather I have mellowed. My daughter-in-law is also annoyingly independent minded and even Eddy has gone off to do his own thing. Not to mention the divorce. Maybe I'm just feeling that it's time for me to change too.'

'It won't be easy.'

I nod.

'How about you? Have you considered retirement?'

'I've told César that I won't hand the business over to him until he gets married.'

'You can't enforce that kind of thing nowadays.'

'I wouldn't if he had more family than just me. But I'm worried he'll be left on his own with nobody to support and cherish him once I'm gone.'

'Have you told him that?'

'Of course. He told me he's too busy to date. I fear it's his bad temper scaring women off.'

'He's rich, a bad temper won't keep women at bay. Would you mind if he dated a man?'

Agata turns to give me her trademark steely glare, then she shakes her head.

'At this point I wouldn't even mind that. Times have changed after all. But I have only ever seen him with women on those rare times he has dated. Unfortunately none have ever lasted very long.'

'At least he dates, I had all but given up hope for Armando to marry, and then he found Diana.'

Agata looks away and I realise that the bride and groom are approaching. Bernardo looks very happy. Far happier than he did at his first marriage, where he'd merely looked star struck. And Maria is glowing.

'We've come to say farewell,' Maria says, always serene, but with a more relaxed smile than usual. 'Thank you for the wonderful reception. It couldn't have been more perfect.'

'I'm glad you liked it,' Agata says standing up to give the bride a kiss to each cheek. 'You look lovely today.'

'And now we're off on our honeymoon,' Bernardo says.

I've also stood up to greet them and he gives me a warm handshake.

'I take it Armando has already left?'

'He and Diana were both looking a little frayed,' Bernardo says.

He knows all about Armando's sensitivity to smell, so he was probably expecting the rapid exit of his best man.

'Well, congratulations. You both look very happy.'

'We are,' Maria says blushing happily and then they hurry off to catch their plane.

'Well, that's that, with the bride and groom gone the party will start to wind down,' Agata says.

Unexpectedly, for one who was eager to leave, I don't want the evening to end. I feel like I've found a new friend, but if we part now nothing will come from it.

Agata flicks a hand in the air that brings a waiter hurrying over.

'Two coffees and a bottle of our best Aguardente Velha,' she says and the waiter leaves with a bow.

'Is that how you intend to send me off?'

I'm hurt but also impressed at Agata's elegant technique.

'I once heard that when a host wants the guests to leave in the Netherlands, they serve them ham and egg sandwiches. A not very subtle way of saying as it's now breakfast time they should go,' Agata says. 'I prefer to end my evenings with a café com cheirinho.'

'Does it not keep you up?'

'The older I've got the less I sleep. It doesn't seem to affect me, either way.'

The waiter returns with a cut crystal decanter containing a rich brown liquid and two gold baroque-style coffee cups that are clearly not part of the hotel stock.

'I'll leave you to determine how much alcohol you'd prefer,' Agata says as she pours a few drops of the aguardente into her coffee and then takes a deep sniff of the blend.

Seeing her look so happy brings a smile to my face. I lean forward over the coffee cup so that she can't see my grin, and give myself a considerably larger dose of the aguardente. The smell is intoxicating on its own, combined with the coffee it reeks of decadence.

'You do know how to treat your guests well,' I say as I take a first sip.

'Of course,' Agata says and leans back in her chair.

She looks like she's perfectly posed for a classical painting.

'Agata, I really enjoyed this chat. Perhaps... you'd go out for a meal with me one day?'

She looks surprised for a moment then she gives a languid smile.

'I would like that.'

Excitement bubbles up inside me making me feel like a teenage boy. How absurd, yet I am glad I made this first move. I have a sense that something special will come of it.

21st December

NAUSICA AND THE NEW JOURNEY

I'm in the passenger seat, gazing numbly at the view. My parents are in the flask-like urn on my lap. We're sharing one last drive.

Pedro, my best friend and constant support over the last few years, is driving. He's the kind of friend who knows when to speak, and when to sit comfortably in silence.

I'm still in shock, although I don't really know why... well, yes, of course I know. I just thought I was better prepared. I've been saying farewell for the last five years, as piece by piece my mother lost everything that made up the complex puzzle of her.

Now I'm watching as the industrial buildings along the Tagus river flash by, then under the massive red steel bridge, past stone monuments to voyages and conquests long gone, parks and riverside walks, cutting-edge galleries beside an ancient power plant. On along the Marginal past the little coves of beaches gradually getting less industrial as the river mouth opens into the Atlantic Ocean. Past palaces and forts and modern blocks of flats, each grand balcony facing the stunning view. It's only just afternoon, but the sun is already low, making me squint against the glare off the water.

For everyone else, this is an ordinary day. Drivers are going about their business, retirees are walking the ocean path and surfers catch the meagre waves. The weather, too, is uncooperative for such a sad day. The sky is a powdery blue dotted with popcorn clouds. The sun is warm and soothing.

We aren't even going on a very long drive. An hour out of Lisbon, maybe an hour and a half. We weave our way past the tourists in Cascais with its quaint fishermen's cottages now turned into millionaires' seaside homes, and out onto the stretch of road that leads to Guincho Beach. This is a long flat stretch of road with cliffs down to the sea on one side and wild sand dunes slowly being colonised by grass and salt-resistant wildflowers.

The air has a golden quality to it and light sparkles off turquoise waves. It's so dazzling I put my sunglasses on, which turns both the sky and the ocean a more intense blue. Pedro slows as we curve past Guincho, where a dune has half consumed the road. The car tyres spin before hitting the tarmac beneath.

Then it's up into the mountains, winding through picturesque villages clinging to the mountainside, pine and sweet chestnut woodland to our right, grassland and cliffs down to the sea far below on our left, an old whitewashed windmill atop a hill.

On and on and I'm slowly relaxing, remembering the last time I took this trip with my mother, and the time before that when I went with Mom and Dad. Tears threaten to well up and I force them down. I'm exhausted from crying. I can't even face that anymore.

To distract myself, I say, 'I got a lot of lovely calls from my ex colleagues at the hospital. I was surprised that so many of them still remembered me.'

'Of course they remembered you,' Pedro says in a deliberately jolly voice. 'You're a great person.'

'That is your opinion, of course.'

'Is there anybody else opinion that matters more to you?' he asks, keeping it playful.

I haven't turned to face him so that he can't see how close I am to crying. I doubt even the sunglasses could hide that.

'No, there's nobody else whose opinion matters to me at all. You are a shining knight and example to me in word and deed.' We've always been like this lavishing praise while pretending we're just kidding. 'Maybe I should follow your example and completely change my profession.'

Pedro used to be a marine biologist, but he had a midlife crisis. He described it as being bored and able to predict exactly what each potential new job in his field would offer him — more of the same. So he took early retirement and became a painter.

His pieces are quirky, often mixing in marine objects. Aside from being his number one fan, I promote him wherever I can. So far, he's making an okay income from his art. More importantly, I've watched him bloom into confident contentment.

'Do you have something in mind?' Pedro asks.

'Not a thing, except it has to involve people.'

'You used to enjoy nursing.'

'Mmm, I still do, although it was increasingly stressful looking after Mom.'

'Geriatric care was never your preferred field.'

'No,' I say as I watch a gull so perfectly balanced as it faces into the wind that it hangs like a kite over the cliffs. 'Oh, that reminds me. Aside from the condolence calls, my old boss got in touch. He said if I wanted a spot back on his surgery team, there would be one.'

'Wow! Is that your weirdo boss, Professor something or other?'

'Genaro, Professor Genaro.'

'He just went straight in to offering you a job? Not a word about your mom?'

'I wouldn't have been surprised if he did that, but no, he started with condolences.'

'So you see, you're such a great nurse people are already calling you up with job offers.'

I laugh. Pedro knows nurses are in short supply and recruiters are always calling from all around the world.

'At least you know you'll never be out of a job. Although I'm not sure you should go back to that odd professor.'

'He wasn't bad, actually.'

'Isn't he one of those genius autistic types, though? I can't imagine them being easy to work with.'

'That's what many people thought. But I noticed he could tell how people were feeling which autistic people struggle with. I think he just found it too exhausting to engage with others' emotions. If you're making life or death decisions every day, it takes its toll.'

'Sounds like you actually like him.'

'I respect him. It wasn't bad being on his team. I was glad that he thought highly enough of me to try to get me back.'

'We're nearly there,' Pedro says.

I turn, taking in the familiar white lighthouse with the red painted room at the top for the light. Our road curves left and down into a car park. Even on a weekday afternoon the carpark is full, mostly with coaches ferrying people to the westernmost tip of Europe, Cabo da Roca.

I gasp as Pedro opens the door and a gust of wind sucks all the warmth away. Then clutching the bag with my parent's ashes, I take hold of Pedro's hand and he helps me out of the car.

Scattering ashes in a nature conservation site or into the ocean is against the law. I was told this quite firmly by the people at the crematorium. Apparently, human remains, even in the form of ash, are considered as toxic waste, although not actually toxic. That's okay, I have no intention of sprinkling my parents' ashes either on land or in the sea. Mom was very clear on the matter.

'Nausica,' she always said, even when most of her other memories and thoughts had long since dissolved, 'I don't want to be scattered or drift aimlessly about. I want to plunge. Put a great big heavy weight in the urn and drop us into the sea so your father and I can form part of a reef for all the little sea creatures.'

And now we're here, walking down the path that takes us to the towering stone monument with the white cross at the top where the tourists are posing for their 'we were here' picture. We continue along the path that hugs the edge of the cliff, the ocean waves crashing far below us, a stiff wind chilling my cheeks and the tip of my nose.

We keep going as the path gets narrower and the people thin out and finally vanish.

'This is a good spot,' I say and take the urn out of my bag. I've put in a couple of heavy garden stones, smooth and rounded because that seemed kinder to my parents.

Pedro checks the path, right and left, and says, 'All clear.'

'I'll miss you, Mom, I'll miss you, Dad,' I say and throw the urn out into the cold blue air. It hangs in space for a moment and then drops so quickly I don't even see the splash as it gets swallowed by a gigantic wave. 'I should have said something more meaningful,' I whisper.

Pedro puts his arm about me and pulls me close.

'It's okay. You said all the meaningful things to them when they were alive. They didn't need any more than that.'

I nod. My eyes are burning but dry.

'Thanks for coming out with me.'

'You couldn't have prevented me from being here.'

'You are so pushy,' I say and give Pedro a playful shove.

Normally, he takes that as his cue to let go. Today, he pulls me even closer.

'Are you ready to go home?'

I take a deep breath, looking around, fixing key features of the landscape in my mind so I don't forget where my parents are. I'm not sure if I will come back. Mom's motto was: You can never go back, nor should you wish to. It got so ingrained, it's become a part of me.

'The house is going to feel very empty,' I say as I start walking, conscious that Pedro is still holding me.

'You can come to mine for a while if you like. Take a day or two to hang out with me before you go home.'

'But there is still so much to do, the will and clearing out mom's house and—'

'Shhh,' Pedro murmurs, 'worry about that tomorrow, or the day after. You've done your one big thing for today. Now you can rest.'

'Do you think so? I've felt... like I've been on the longest marathon run and I've just started up a particularly steep hill.'

Pedro stops, puts a hand on each shoulder and peers so long and hard at my face that I start to feel awkward.

'What are you doing?'

'Trying to decide on something,' he says and starts walking again.

'Something like what?' I ask, hurrying to catch up.

'Like whether I'm a fool for waiting or a fool to say something.'

'Either way, you're just being foolish, so spit it out.'

This hesitant Pedro is unfamiliar and I don't like it.

'Nausica, do you realise how much I like you?'

'Of course I do. I like you too.'

'No, more than that,' he says, his words being whipped away by the stiff ocean breeze. 'I've wanted to tell you for a long time, but it never felt like the right time. First your work was all-consuming, then your father's illness and your mother's dementia, and now... I probably shouldn't be saying this when you're so emotionally fragile but you talking about a marathon made me realise there are still more obstacles ahead. So I suppose it's now or never.'

I stop and take the sunglasses off, as if that will help me understand better.

'What are you saying?'

'I love you. I have done for years.'

My mind's a blank. How can Pedro be saying this to me now? How can he ruin our wonderful friendship with this preposterous...

'I always hoped that the reason you stayed single,' Pedro said, 'was that there wasn't a man you liked better than me.'

Was that the reason? My ability to think has turned to treacle. I'm too tired for this kind of shock.

But then I realise Pedro is my rock. I used to say that as a joke because of his name, but it's always been true. During my darkest times, he's stood firm, always there for me. And I've always been there when he needed me too, mending wounds, both physical and emotional.

'We are pretty good together, aren't we?'

'I've always thought so.'

I hold out my hand, and he takes it in a tight grip and pulls me closer. Then, to my surprise and pleasure, he kisses me.

I laugh. He leans back grinning.

'I can't tell you how long it's been since I've wanted to do that.'

I wrap my arm around his waist and say, 'I may not know what I'll be doing with myself from now on, but at least I know one thing. Whatever it is, I'll be doing it with you.'

Pedro gives his trademark shout of pleasure, then turns me to the west, looking out over the ocean where the sun has begun to set.

'Let's remember this moment together forever.'

The sky has turned a burned orange, the few clouds picked out in brilliant yellow. I snuggle deeper into Pedro's embrace, realising that I've always loved the smell of him. This day might be ending in brilliant flaming colours, but our new life together is just beginning.

22nd December

CARLOS AND THE MISSING CAT

I've been away too long. Even though Christmas is going to be a quiet one since most of my extended family live in other countries. I'm really looking forward to snuggling up with my newest family member, a little stray black cat I took in during the summer.

It's astonishing how such a small creature has made such an enormous impact in my life. Especially as I wasn't a pet kind of person and have never had one before. Merry just moved in, as if giving me a stamp of feline approval. I didn't just accept that, though. I went around the neighbourhood trying to find his owner, put up posters everywhere, including all the local vets. He wasn't chipped, but I can definitely say I tried my best to find his original family.

Most of my friends and neighbours though were sure he was a stray who'd just found a soft touch to give him a forever home. Whatever the truth, Merry and I bonded within days.

When I was working, he'd curl up in my wicker in-tray, or, if he felt ignored, he'd plonk himself on my keyboard. When I was reading or watching TV, he'd settle himself in a proprietary way on my lap or curled up under my chin. For someone who can't speak, he sure does provide a lot of company.

I'm a photographer for a fashion company that's just moved from Milan. I spend my days taking glamour shots of extraordinarily beautiful women. Now I've replaced two of my best photos with shots of Merry. One has pride of place in my entrance hall, the other in the bedroom. He gives all those women a run for their money.

So, when I had to go to Milan for another shoot, I was in the unaccustomed position of having to find somebody to look after my cat. After much research, recommendations and angst, I found Paula. She was highly recommended by my new circle of pet-owning friends and, most importantly, Merry liked her.

Merry has a habit of vanishing when I have friends over. I want to show him off, but you could swear I don't even have a cat when he makes himself scarce. But he came out to inspect Paula.

She was a slim, unimposing woman, with her hair scraped back into a ponytail and a beanie over the lot. But she had the good sense to arrive with cat treats. Merry probably came out for the treats, she'd said with a laugh. But he'd also allowed her to give him a little scratch under the chin. So I went off, confident that he'd be comfortable and safe without me.

Paula was great and sent me photos every day of Merry, eating, sleeping or enjoying the view from my apartment. I really looked forward to the daily update and Paula's cheery texts about what Merry had been up to. She also always calls me Merry's dad, which I found strange but is apparently quite common amongst lovers of cats and dogs.

I really enjoyed getting those texts and not only for the news about Merry. Paula has quite the sense of humour. I even took to quipping back between shoots. Our exchanges felt like the comfortable banter of old friends.

Then, the day before I was due back home, Paula asked what I was bringing Merry for Christmas. The thought of buying a pet a present hadn't entered my head. But now, here I am, the taxi crawling through the narrow streets of Lisbon, with a cat toy wrapped in colourful paper and with a flashy ribbon. The pet shop owner had not only not thought it was a strange thing to do, but appeared to think it was exactly what should be done.

I paid the taxi driver, and looked up at the lights on in my apartment. My heart quickened in anticipation as I dragged my suitcase into the foyer and pressed the call button on the elevator.

That was when I heard a soft voice echo down the stairs, 'Merry, Merry,' followed by 'psss, psss, psss.'

A horrible premonition shook me. Never have I felt such dread, and I hurried to the steps and called up.

'Ms Paula? Ms Paula, is that you?'

'Mr Carlos?' came back the vaguely familiar voice.

Then there was a clattering of steps as she charged down the stairs and arrived breathless and frazzled before me.

'Oh, Mr Carlos, I can't find Merry!'

The feeling of doom that had settled upon me intensified.

'What do you mean?'

'He didn't come for his food when I called him at 4pm, which isn't like him. So I searched the apartment, shaking the bag of treats and he didn't come out.'

'Where have you looked?'

'Everywhere,' Paula says in despair. 'I checked all the cupboards, even though I hadn't opened any, under the beds and the rest of the furniture, in the bathrooms, the laundry basket, inside the washing machine and the dishwasher. And when I didn't find him, I looked everywhere all over again.'

'So what could have happened?' I ask because I can't imagine where Merry might have got to either after hearing this exhaustive list.

'Well…' Paula says, while wringing her hands. 'I opened the window to air the apartment around midday, and a little after two pm there was a delivery for you. I am sure he didn't slip out during either of those two moments, but I can't think what else might have happened.'

'So now?'

'I've just been checking all the floors, in case he's somewhere in the common area. Maybe you want to call him outside the building. He's more likely to come if he hears your voice than if he hears mine.'

I feel an irrational rage building up inside me at this woman. How could she have been so careless as to have lost my cat? I have a sick feeling in the pit of my stomach too at the thought of never seeing Merry again. My mind is filled with awful images of what might have happened to my little black friend if he did go outside.

No, I say to myself, be sensible. Merry lived out on the streets before he charmed his way into your life. He can look after himself. He'll be okay. So I abandon my suitcase beside the elevator and, making sure no black cat goes streaking out, I open the main door. Then, still checking, I close it behind myself and start calling for Merry.

Paula stays inside, calling and looking behind the collection of potted plants in the foyer. I walk up the street shouting Merry's name and looking inside bins and under each of the parked cars that make the road so narrow you can barely drive a car through it. The one advantage of that is that cars can't build up much speed. But still I'm looking along the pavement for any dead or injured cats. The sick feeling builds inside me as I work myself up a couple of blocks and then go downhill for an additional few blocks.

The research I'd done on cats when I was trying to find Merry's original owners had said that cats will easily travel over 10 kilometres a night when out foraging. I decide I'll work out that range and walk every street. I'll leave no stone unturned to find Merry.

But first, I should send Paula home. There isn't anything more she can do and as my despair grows, I will find it harder to speak to her. It isn't her fault. I leave my windows open throughout the summer and Merry has never gone out of them before. He also runs and hides when the doorbell buzzes, so I can't really blame Paula.

'I think it's best you go home,' I say.

'I'm so sorry,' Paula whispers, and can't even make eye contact as we travel up in the lift.

Unfortunately, she has to collect her handbag. I open the apartment door with a feeling of despair to be returning to an empty home. Paula picks up her handbag, which is resting against a battered cardboard box. Presumably today's delivery. The postman has not treated it well, and the cardboard has ripped over two corners.

'Well...' Paula says, giving me a wan look.

'Meow?' comes a little voice and Merry's head pops out of the cardboard box.

'Merry!' I yell as he hops out of the box and approaches me with his tail pointing straight up and quivering excitedly. I scoop him into my arms, kissing his face as wave after exquisite wave of relief washes over me. 'You gave me such a fright.'

'The box!' Paula said. 'I never thought to look in there.'

'I'm not surprised,' I say, scratching Merry's head to make sure he really is there. 'The little so and so was probably sleeping happily, ignoring the world while we were running around like maniacs calling for him.'

'Such a typical cat,' Paula says, as she also gives Merry's head a little scratch. She's looking as relieved as I am.

'I think we could both use a cup of calming tea,' I say. 'Would you like to stay for a bit?'

'Thank you, yes,' Paula says, the last bit of guilt and tension fading from her face.

I'm glad Merry's fine, and I'm glad that means I'll be seeing Paula again. I'd been thinking so whenever I got one of her texts. Hopefully, one day soon, Merry and I will become her two favourite males.

23rd December

A GIFT FOR JACINTA

My phone gives a loud ping and I jump because I am so focused on the on-line auction. I reach for the phone, intending to put it on silent. I'm a personal shopper and Christmas is my busiest time. I'm rammed to the ceiling with last-minute orders and don't have time to take on anyone else. But the message on the lock screen nearly stops my heart.

The brooch is on sale!

'Shit!' I scream.

The brooch! The one I've been trying to get my hands on for years only to be blocked by my father every time.

I punch the air a dozen times as I leap out of my chair. It sends the mouse flying, but I don't have time to pick it up. I'm scrambling out of my pyjamas as I dash to the wardrobe. No time to be picky. I slip on a sweatshirt with a long defunct pop band's name emblazoned across the chest and hop on one foot to get my jeans, accordioned in a heap on the floor, on.

'Hey, Siri,' I yell. You have to yell at Siri, otherwise she doesn't respond. 'Call Liliana.'

'Calling Liliana,' my phone intones as I snatch up my bag and dig about in it.

No point going after a treasure if I arrive without money.

'Hello?' comes Liliana's far too calm voice.

'Lili, are you sure it's on sale?' I shout as I flip piles of papers stacked on my desk over, looking for my purse.

'Would I make a mistake about that? It's at the Lusíadas Jewellers.'

'Thanks, Hon, I owe you one,' I say as I chuck the phone into my bag while running to the front door.

I palm my car keys. I'm too impatient to wait for the lift in my apartment so I take the stairs and then run down the road to where the car is ramped up on the pavement under a dripping tree.

'Calm down, calm down,' I mutter to myself as, with shaking hands, I push the key into the ignition and the car starts with a roar.

I ease myself into the heavy Lisbon traffic. Everyone is out last-minute shopping and every last one of them is determined to get in my way. It takes forever to drive the dozen blocks to the shopping mall.

It's one of the older malls in Lisbon, so it's smaller than the modern ones but just as crowded. We're all being jollied along by blaring Christmas pop. I thread my way through and try not to push anyone, but a certain amount of jostling is inevitable.

I turn the corner and hurry past Santa's grotto and a long line of eager-looking kids and tired helper elves to the discreet gold sign of the Lusíadas' Jewellers. I also spot an all too familiar figure a half a dozen steps ahead of me heading in the same direction.

'No!' I gasp.

I might only see his back, but those shapely shoulders can't be hidden, even in a baggy, dark green woollen coat. It's Oceano, and he can only be here for one thing. I push the woman dawdling in front of me out of the way so hard she staggers sideways, then I run.

Oceano still gets through the door ahead of me. Worse, he's heading towards the counter with his hand already raised to get the assistant's attention.

'Yes, sir, can I help you?' the woman asks, approaching him with a professional smile.

'No!' I gasp as I slam my hand on the counter.

Oceano turns to look down at me and says in his all too familiar cool voice that has always driven me crazy, once because I loved it so much and now because I hate it, 'Hello, Jacinta.'

'It's mine,' I say, panting.

'What is?'

'You know damn well what I'm talking about, the brooch!'

Oceano just smiles at me, then turns to the attendant.

'Do you have the item I called ahead for? My name is Oceano Furtado.'

'Of course, Mr Oceano, just one minute please,' the woman says and beats a hasty retreat.

'Oceano, you didn't,' I whisper, impotent rage washing over me. 'Please tell me you aren't here for the brooch.'

'I don't know what you're talking about,' Oceano says, giving me a bland smile.

He's always been better than me at hiding how he really feels and I'm helpless against his Herculean immovability. It was one reason for our breakup.

The attendant comes back with a red velvet box and, with great ceremony, eases the lid open. Nestled within the folds of tan satin is an ornate brooch with clusters of semi-precious gems in an avant-garde gold and silver setting.

'You didn't,' I say and my voice sinks to a whisper as the blood and all my pent up energy drains away. 'Not this brooch, please, Oceano.'

'It's exquisite,' he says, sounding particularly cool and disinterested.

Oceano is a jewellery designer. We met when I commissioned a piece from him for an exceptionally difficult client. We were immediately drawn to each other, and I moved in with him within the first month.

Hindsight is a great thing, but I guess you couldn't say it was entirely a mistake because we spent three tumultuous years together. We broke up because he said I was too secretive and I accused him of being too nosy. I can't say I left without regrets, but now, after a year of not seeing him, to meet again under these circumstances is heart-breaking.

'You have to let me buy that brooch.'

I try to keep the pleading note out of my voice. I don't succeed. Oceano gives me his calculating look, and my fears about this encounter grow.

'If this gift is for somebody really important and you can convince me of the fact, I will give it up to you.'

Yep, that's it. He's prying again. Why can't he just accept what I have to say, that the brooch is important to me?

'Why do you want it?' I say as a challenge.

Maybe I can convince him without giving in.

'It's a beautiful design. I'm going to add it to my inspiration collection.'

I don't believe him, although it could be true. Oceano collects interesting and unique pieces to learn from and gain inspiration. This brooch certainly fits that category. But his answer just doesn't ring true.

'Now stop stalling. If you want this brooch, you're going to have to give me a truthful answer.'

His question stings. He always worried that I was lying to him. I wasn't, mostly I was evading, but with good reason. It was such an ingrained response that I couldn't even bring myself to explain that either.

I pull myself up to my full height, look Oceano straight in the eye and say with all sincerity, 'It's a gift to myself. So I can tell you I really want it. How many gifts have you received from other people that you've not cared a jot about? No gift is more important than the one you give yourself.'

Oceano gives me a cynical smile.

'I should have known you wouldn't tell me.' Then he turns to the assistant and says. 'Wrap it up for me.'

'Oceano, please,' I say, and my heart is beating a desperate, unsteady tap dance.

This is a nightmare. It can't be happening.

'At least you'll know where the brooch is now,' he says, and his demeanour softens. 'If you ever decide to be honest with me, I'll give you the brooch.'

'This is crazy.'

I'm embarrassed that the assistant is standing behind the counter listening in. Even if she is looking uncomfortable to be there. Oceano holds out his card, and she whips out the payment machine so quickly she's obviously keen to see the back of us.

I watch with increasing despair as the brooch is placed in a pretty Lusíadas Jewellery box, then wrapped with a ribbon placed in a fancy paper bag and handed over with great ceremony to Oceano.

I follow him out of the jeweller's and into the crowds of Christmas shoppers. He's just ruined my day, no, maybe my life. I chide myself for being overly dramatic, but my heart is breaking.

I trail after him, but the distance between us gradually increases until I can barely see him amongst the other shoppers. This is my fault, I think as tears prick my eyes. He gave me a chance, and I didn't take it.

Thinking back, he was always trying to crack my defensive walls. But why now? Why, after we've already gone our separate ways?

I take out my phone and text Liliana.

I didn't get it. I was too late.

Oh, I'm sorry, Honey. Do you know who got it? Maybe you can offer them a deal?

That's typical Liliana. She's a businesswoman through and through. She says no deal is ever absolutely closed. Today she's wrong.

No chance, I'm afraid.

Do you want me to come over and beat the buyer up for you? It could be cathartic?

It's Oceano.

There's a longer pause in the text coming back, so I know she's surprised.

Maybe he has a good reason for wanting it.

He's going to use it for inspiration.

Are you sure that's all?

I stare at my phone in surprise. Liliana was my fiercest supporter when I broke up with Oceano. Now this? Then again, she has a new boyfriend, the first since university, and an old foe to boot. She's feeling all loved up and seeing the world through the proverbial rose-tinted spectacles.

I look through the crowds, certain Oceano will be long gone. To my surprise, I spot him sitting at a cafe table that juts out into the busy walkway. That is entirely unlike him. He hates malls, he hates crowds, and he'd rather chop off an arm than stop for a drink in such a busy, noisy space.

The waitress threads her way towards him and deposits a coffee and French toast. It's my favourite Christmas treat. Oceano doesn't like sweets. That man is definitely waiting for me. I'm actually nauseous because he's made me so nervous.

I push my way through the crowd, put my hand on the back of the chair opposite his and say, 'Is this free?'

He smiles up at me, and it's his kind smile that used to melt my heart. So he knows the pain he's putting me through. He pushes the toast across to me.

'Would you like a coffee too?'

I shake my head. I couldn't eat or drink a drop. Not now. I've come this far and I have to screw up my courage and try to get this done. Oceano is a man of his word. If he says he'll give me the brooch in exchange for a confession, he means it.

'That brooch,' I say, keeping my gaze fixed on the table, the French toast a blur on the edge of my vision. 'It belonged to my mother.' I can't look up, so I don't know how Oceano is reacting. Nor do I care.

'She left it for me. It was the only thing she left after she ran away from my father. He knew how much I loved the brooch, but that bastard kept it from me. And now it looks like he sold it instead of giving it to me.'

'It's from his estate,' Oceano said. 'He died.'

'What?' I ask and look up because I'm so surprised.

'You didn't know?'

'I wanted nothing to do with him after I grew up.'

Oceano nodded.

'How do you even know about him?' I ask, my suspicion brimming over.

'After we broke up...' Ocean says then pauses as if gathering his thoughts. 'I always suspected your childhood was messed up. The way you refused to speak about your parents. The way you always changed the subject if I suggested we meet them, or when I mentioned marriage. So after we broke up, I needed to know why. I needed to understand what I did wrong. I couldn't find your mother, but I met your father. He seemed nice enough.'

I shudder. I don't want to talk about my father. Especially as that was what the world thought about him. He seemed like a perfectly pleasant man who had the misfortune of having his wife run away and dumping his daughter on him. The saint who cared for his poor abandoned Jacinta.

'He was far from nice.'

'I realised that. You were always drawing pictures of that brooch, so I asked him about it and he turned quite nasty.'

Oceano must have been too pushy. Like he was with me, probing away. It would have been enough to make the man snap.

'Did he beat you and your mother?'

'He never raised a finger to us. The man didn't have to. He had a hurtful way with words. He could also manipulate you into thinking black was white, hate was love, that my mother was ungrateful.'

I shrug.

Even now that I'm finally saying these things, the pain of those years of manipulation is almost too much to confront, especially with Oceano. He pushes the jeweller's bag across the table to me.

'Sorry I did this to you. Sorry I pushed you so hard. I really missed you and regretted so much of what I did. I wanted some way to see you again.'

'And to probe some more?'

'I'm sorry about that too,' Oceano says, reaches across and squeezes my hand. 'It was wrong of me to prod at such a painful wound.'

His touch is like static electricity, shocking, painful but a necessary jolt.

'I missed you too,' I say, tears spilling from my eyes. 'It was just so hard. I always knew I should tell you more. That I should explain, but I couldn't. I just couldn't.'

Oceano leaps up and wraps me in a hug. I bury my face in his chest.

'Now that I know, do you think we could try again?'

'Really?' I say as I tighten my grip on Oceano.

'We can go slow. Not rush into things like we did last time.'

'Maybe do things a bit differently?'

'I will be more respectful of your boundaries.'

I laugh.

'Like you were today?'

'I'm sorry about that.'

I let go and look up at Oceano. He seems more uncertain than I've ever seen him. For some reason, that reassures me.

'I suppose I should thank you. I missed you so much too, but I was afraid to make contact again. Your shock tactic may have broken through a barrier I would never have crossed without a push. But don't you dare do that ever again.'

'I promise I won't,' Oceano says and pulls me into an even tighter hug.

I finally relax. I've been holding my breath for the last year, struggling on in misery. Today I got my second chance at happiness.

24th December

ARMANDO'S CHRISTMAS EVE SURPRISE

*H*e's arrived!

I'm texting using one hand because Diana is still gripping the other tight. The congratulatory texts start pinging back, giving me a fright because I thought the phone was on silent. I hastily mute it, but can't help grinning from ear to ear to see all the messages from friends.

Then I call my father.

'He's here,' I whisper, 'Noel Mafeu Luna Zeller.'

'Eh? Noel?'

The plan had been to name him after my grandfather, Mafeu.

'It just seemed the right name under the circumstances.'

Noel arrived earlier than expected. He was due in two weeks' time. We were just getting ready to go on our last holiday as a couple when Diana went into labour. Fortunately, she's the kind to plan ahead. She already had her hospital bag packed. I was in such a panic that I forgot the bag and had to go running back into the house to fetch it.

Despite attending all the pre-birth classes, I realised that while we were mentally prepared for the birth. I was far from emotionally prepared. I have never felt more helpless in the face of Diana's suffering.

I was shaken to the core, and am still feeling wobbly hours afterwards. Even though everything went well, and the doctors and nurses have told us we have a healthy baby boy.

The moment they gave him to Diana to hold, she gave a startled little, 'Oh!' and her face took on the softest, most loving expression I have ever seen.

That was when I realised she had truly become a mother. I thought I couldn't love her more, but at that moment, my heart really felt like it would burst as I gazed down upon her and our son.

'It's going to be a surreal Christmas,' I say as I open the front door to let Diana in.

She's carrying the tiny car seat in which Noel is sleeping peacefully.

'To think it was going to be out last Christmas alone.'

'That didn't quite go to plan.'

'Did you remember to cancel our reservation?'

'All done and no quibbles after I told them about Noel.'

I couldn't actually stop myself. I came over all proud father and was babbling away about it even after the hotel had offered me a full refund.

Diana, in the meantime, has settled herself on the sofa. She still looks pale and was walking with a slight limp, but she's also serene. She looks a lot calmer than I feel as she puts the car seat on the sofa beside her and runs a fingertip gently over Noel's tiny cheek.

He's looking a lot better than yesterday. I didn't want to say anything at the time, but he was so red and blotchy and wrinkled that I'd worried something had gone badly wrong. Now his skin is smooth and has a healthy natural pink glow, and his head is covered in a fine down of black hair. He looks ridiculously cute.

'Can I get you anything?' I ask Diana.

The doctors pronounced her fit to go home, but to rest for the next few days. The nurses gave me strict instructions to look after her and not let her do too much too soon. It was my intention anyway, although Diana has steely resolve and will do as she pleases whatever I say.

'We don't even have anything in the house,' she says, leaning back on the sofa and curling her feet under herself.

'Don't worry, I've arranged all of that.'

'How? All the takeaways will be shut or too busy and you don't like the smell from them, anyway.'

'Not takeaway,' I say as I bring Diana a glass of milk. 'Not that kind, anyway.'

'And milk?'

'I was told you need to be given something easy to digest, and the nurse said milk is good. It's also one of the few things we still have in the fridge.'

'How about wine?' Diana says, giving me a cheeky grin.

She's been craving wine for the last nine months and had vowed to drink a glass of red the moment she came home. That was before Noel. Now she seems less interested.

The doorbell trills and we both check on Noel first, catch each other doing it and laugh. How quickly priorities change.

'That will be our Christmas lunch.'

Eddy is on the other side of the intercom, grinning via the camera and holding up a tartan thermos bag. I let him in and he grabs me in a bear hug.

'Congratulations, bro'! I can't believe you're finally a dad.'

'You realise that makes you an uncle, right?' I say, beaming.

'Uncle Eddy, I can't wait to hear the kid call me that. Where is my nephew?'

'Living room.'

'I brought a bolo rei. It was the least smelly thing I could find.'

I've got better at coping with strong smells. I still avoid them, but I realised the migraines they brought on had more to do with the stress of being bombarded by smells than the smell itself. It means I've relaxed about that and can bear to have more smells in my house than I used to.

'Although,' Eddy says over his shoulder, 'I expect babies are pretty smelly little beings.'

'So I've heard.'

'No, stay down,' Eddy says as he leans down to give Diana a kiss to each cheek before turning his full attention to his nephew. 'He's so tiny!' he whispers, gazing down at Noel with a mix of adoration and amazement that I approve of.

I only have time to put the cake, and bottles of champagne that Eddy hadn't mentioned but seem appropriate, down, before the doorbell trills again.

This time it's Elena. Her turning up is a surprise. I'd expected a congratulatory email at most from my half-sister.

'Hello,' I say as I let her in. 'It's good of you to come.'

'Well... it is Christmas, and I have become an aunt, after all.'

To my surprise, she hands me two paper bags. One has a container with what looks like leitão and a bag of freshly baked bread. The other is a little box, wrapped in Christmas paper and tied with a red bow.

'For the baby.' Elena is looking increasingly embarrassed. 'My PA bought it. I have no idea what it is, but he tends to be sensible.'

'So he's working out, is he?' I hope this is a mild enough question to not raise Elena's hackles. I'd noticed she'd taken her PA to Bernardo's wedding with the excuse that they had some work to do.

'He's fine,' she says, but her brows pull together in irritation.

'Diana's in the living room. You go ahead.'

At least Elena and Diana get on. I wouldn't say they're close, but she doesn't have the enmity towards Diana that she does towards me. I'm hoping, for the first time in my life, that maybe our relationship can improve.

There's no time to think about it now though, as Margarida and Fernando are making their way up the drive. Fernando is weighted down with a multitude of bags, but somehow still able to hang onto Margarida's hand.

Margarida is Diana's best friend, and the closest thing to family Diana has. Although Diana did call her free spirited mother to give her the good news. She's never around, even when Diana was growing up, but she seemed thrilled to learn she'd become a grandmother.

Less thrilling is Fernando, who is Diana's ex. Thankfully he has now switched his affection to Margarida, but I never thought I'd be welcoming him into my home.

'Congratulations!' Margarida says long before she reaches the door. 'I'm so excited. How is Diana?'

'Very well,' I say while returning her enthusiastic kisses. 'But see if you can get her to sit still as the doctor ordered and not get up to greet all the guests.'

'You can count on me.'

Margarida winks like a conspirator and I leave them to go in because my father has turned up. My mother is trailing along just behind him and it looks like they came together. This is surprising since they've been divorced for nearly thirty years. They are also both weighed down with parcels.

'Congratulations!' my father says, slapping my shoulder. 'I couldn't be prouder.'

It's funny that at my age my father's words still please me.

'I can't believe it either. I thought it would never happen,' my mother says.

She's all about the money and had ordered me, just before I met Diana, to get married to ensure I got my hands on the lion's share of the inheritance. It wasn't something I had been worried about. A perverse part of me wishes she hadn't got her way.

'Yes, alright, grandma. Come in and meet your grandson.'

'Armando, no! Never mention the G word. I'm far too young for that. By the way, will Bernardo be here?'

Bernardo is my best friend and normally would have come, but for one detail.

'He's in the Maldives on his honeymoon. Much as he's going to love his new Godson, even he wouldn't drop everything to be here today.'

I'm finally done with door duty and follow my parents into what used to be my spotlessly clean, minimalist sitting room. True, Diana has added some colour and her own touches with the furniture she brought with her, but now the room is full of people all talking in hushed voices, while leaning over little Noel, burbling in baby voices.

He's woken up and is staring out into the world with an adorable, awed expression. Packages, gifts and wrapping paper surround Diana and Noel. Elena and Margarida are busy setting the table with a feast's-worth of food. It looks like everyone bagged up their Christmas meals and brought them over.

Who would have thought that my family would pull together in this way? All I'd asked was for them to bring a little something for Diana and me when they came to visit Noel. I hadn't expected a whole celebratory meal, nor this warm glow that has settled on everyone.

My father looks thrilled and is going on about how Noel looks just like I did as a baby, and my mother is actually nodding in agreement. My sister looks perfectly happy even though for a guilty moment I realise I haven't told her and Eddy's mother about Noel. She'd brought me up, but not kindly, so I avoid her.

'She's on holiday in Morocco with her new boyfriend,' Eddy says in an undertone as he hands me a glass of champagne.

'How did you know what I was thinking?'

'You were looking at Elena and your expression suddenly became alarmed. But honestly, it's best she isn't here for your sake and dad's.'

It's an amazing Christmas. The most family-like one I've ever experienced. Everyone has a grin plastered across their face, and they're all speaking quietly so as not to disturb Noel, who drifts in and out of sleep, cuddled in Diana's arms. She's looking tired, though, and is still very pale. I notice Elena watching her too, and then our eyes meet.

'We should probably get going,' she says and stands up. 'You look like you could use some rest.'

Margarida, who'd been chatting away animatedly to Diana, pulls herself up short.

'Absolutely right. We'll just tidy up and then leave the two of you in peace.'

I've never seen a more efficient, or hushed, tidying up, as everyone hurries to help.

'We have put everything into meal-sized tubs,' Eddy says giving me a farewell hug and another back thumping. 'It should keep you going for a couple of days. Now we'd best be off. The big fathering job is all yours!'

The rest of the family offer similar good wishes.

Elena stops at the door and says, 'Congratulations. For everything.'

For the first time, I'm feeling that our relationship might have a chance of improving. It's amazing what our little baby miracle is achieving.

I hurry back to Diana, who's returned to the sofa, cradling Noel.

'Peace at last,' I say as I settle and put my arm around Diana.

'It was very kind of them to come. We felt like a proper family.'

'We did. It's all thanks to our little boy,' I say as I draw Diana even closer, Noel nestling between us. I give him a peck to his forehead, then give Diana a proper kiss.

'Best Christmas ever,' I say.

Enjoyed this book? You can make a huge difference
If you enjoyed the book please take a moment to let people know why. The review can be as short as you like.

Thank you very much!
If you'd like to read about how Armando and Diana got together buy the novel: Scent of Love.

Get my short story collection Shorties for FREE!

Sign up for my no-spam newsletter that only goes out when there is a new book or freebie available and get my collection of short stories for free, at: https://substack.com/@marinapacheco

Find out more about me and all my books: www.marinapacheco.me

Also By

Get all my books here:

MEDIEVAL HISTORICAL FICTION ePub, paperback and hardback

Fraternity of Brothers, *Life of Galen, Book 1* – Cast out for a crime committed against him, his future looks bleak. Until an unexpected visitor gives him hope for justice. A fight for acceptance, absolution and friendship in Anglo-Saxon England.

Comfort of Home, *Life of Galen, Book 2* – Proven innocent, he's returned from exile. Can he recover all that he lost? A tale of friendship and return to a family he thought he'd lost, set in Anglo-Saxon England.

Kindness of Strangers, *Life of Galen, Book 3* – Trapped in a land plagued by vikings, can one small miracle be all they need to survive? A tale of miracles, betrayal and friendship while under viking siege.

The King's Hall, *Life of Galen, Book 4* – As if being commissioned to create a book to turn back the Apocalypse isn't enough, intrigue and romance threaten to destroy everything he's come to rely upon. Friendship, love and intrigue at the court of King Aethelred the Unready.

Restless Sea, *Life of Galen, Book 5* – Just when they thought they could go home, they're thrust into an adventure at sea. A journey that tests the bonds of friendship.

Friend of My Enemy, *Life of Galen, Book 6* – Captured by an implacable enemy, their future looks bleak. Will escape even be possible?

Road to Rome, *Life of Galen, Book 7* — A journey across a turbulent continent. Will Galen find the answers he seeks?

Eternal City, *Life of Galen, Book 8* — Galen and Alcuin delve into the secrets of the corrupt and decaying city of Medieval Rome.

AUDIOBOOKS narrated by Jacob Daniels
Fraternity of Brothers, *Life of Galen, Book 1*
Comfort of Home, *Life of Galen, Book 2*
Kindness of Strangers, *Life of Galen, Book 3*
The King's Hall, *Life of Galen, Book 4*
  Restless Sea, *Life of Galen, Book 5*

HISTORICAL ROMANCE: ePub, paperback, hardback and audiobooks with AI narration
Sanctuary, *a sweet Medieval mystery* – He needs shelter. She wants a way out. Will his brave move to protect risk both their hearts? An optimistic tale of redemption with heart-warming characters and feel-good thrills.

The Duke's Heart, *a sweet Victorian romance* – His body may be weak, but his dreams know no bounds. Will she be the answer to his prayers? A disabled duke, a strong and determined woman and a slow-building relationship.

Duchess in Flight, *a swashbuckling romance* – She's on the run from a deadly enemy. He lives in the shadows of truth. When their lives merge, will their battle for survival lead to love? A reluctant hero, a woman and her children in distress, a chase to the death.

What the Pauper Did, *a body swap mystery romance* – How do you define yourself? Is it through your appearance, your memories or your soul? Intrigue, murder and romance in an alternate Lisbon of 1770.

CONTEMPORARY ROMANCE ePub, paperback, hardback and audiobooks with AI narration
Scent of Love – Can two polar opposite perfumers overcome their differences and create a unique blend all of their own? Love, intrigue and clashing values in the perfume houses of Lisbon. □
Sky Therapy — A detective and the son of a serial killer. Is it safest to stay apart, or will they risk everything for love? □
Terapia Celeste — My first novel (Sky Therapy) to be translated into Brazilian Portuguese.

SCIENCE FICTION/ FANTASY ePub and paperback
City of Night, *Eternal City, Book 1* – World-threatening danger, a female demonologist, an unwitting apprentice, a city in a single tower, a satisfying ending.

SHORT STORIES: ePub, paperback, and AI narration
Living, Loving, Longing, Lisbon, Vol 1 & Vol 2 – A collection of short stories inspired by the city of Lisbon, written by people from around the world who live in, visited or love Lisbon.□
Loves of Lisbon – A Christmas advent calendar of 24 short, sweet romances of the intertwining lives of the residents of Lisbon.□

FREEBIES: ePub and AI narration
Shorties – My shortest works: futuristic, contemporary and historical available for free when you sign up to my newsletter.

About Author

Marina Pacheco a binge writer of historical fiction, sweet romance, sci-fi and fantasy novels as well as short stories. She writes easy reading, feel-good novels that are perfect for a commute or to curl up with on a rainy day. She currently lives on the coast just outside Lisbon, after stints in London, Johannesburg, and Bangkok, which all sounds more glamorous than it actually was. Her ambition is to publish 100 books. This is taking considerably longer than she'd anticipated! □

You can find out more about Marina Pacheco's work, and download several freebies, on her website: https://marinapacheco.me □
Website: https://marinapacheco.me
    Sign up to Marina's newsletter via her website or on Substack to keep up to date on all her writing activities, get early previews of covers and first chapters, short stories and freebies.□
Follow me on substack: https://substack.com/@marinapacheco
email: hi@marinapacheco.me

Milton Keynes UK
Ingram Content Group UK Ltd.
UKHW030859151124
451262UK00001B/52